£3

THE SILENCE
OF COLONEL BRAMBLE
and
THE DISCOURSES
OF DOCTOR O'GRADY

Uniform with this volume

ANDRÉ MAUROIS

Ariel: A Shelley romance
The Art of Living
The Art of Writing
Byron
Disraeli

ANDRÉ MAUROIS

The Silence
of Colonel Bramble
and
The Discourses of
Doctor O'Grady

THE BODLEY HEAD
LONDON

Les Silences du Colonel Bramble
First published in Great Britain 1919

Les Discours du Dr O'Grady
First published in Great Britain 1921

This edition containing both first published 1965

All rights reserved
Foreword to this edition © André Maurois 1965
Printed and bound in Great Britain for
The Bodley Head Ltd
10 Earlham Street, London, WC2
by C. Tinling & Co. Ltd, Prescot
Set in Monotype Plantin

CONTENTS

Author's Foreword, 7

The Silence of Colonel Bramble, 15

Appendix: The verse in the original, 145

The Discourses of Doctor O'Grady, 157

AUTHOR'S
FOREWORD TO NEW EDITION

1915–1965. It will be fifty years ago this year, while I was moving from Béthune to Bailleul, from Poperinghe to Ypres with the IXth Scottish Division, that I started a little book which was going to be called *Les Silences du Colonel Bramble*. I kept a notebook, and the conversations I heard over meals in the Officers' Mess seemed to me so unusual, and on occasions so revealing, that I would often jot down a word or a whole sentence by way of committing to memory some anecdote, some discussion.

Little by little there emerged from this hard life an insane aching poetry. It appeared to me first in musical guise. Evening after evening the colonel's gramophone ran through the same songs, *Destiny Waltz*, *Pack up your troubles in your old kit-bag*; then came the violin, Kreisler's, and the voice of Caruso. The songs emanated from the gramophone against a sustained bass-note of cannon and small arms fire. Outside, the flares slowly rose and fell. The machine-guns stuttered. Round the table the faces dreamed of some distant English countryside, of a woman, a career. It was melancholy, poignant and beautiful.

'If only,' I thought, 'if only one could capture all this! This monotony, this rhythm of war, these refrains in which love and death are blended . . . Perhaps then one could write a book which would be the very image of these men, of this land . . .'

And as I listened for the hundredth time to *Destiny Waltz*, I mentally assayed expressions which took on in spite of me the form of poems. The colonel would watch me uneasily as I wrote down lines of short extent.

'Are you a poet?' he asked, suspiciously.

In all sincerity I replied: 'No, sir.'

Reassured, he would relapse into his silence—for my colonel of the time had several of the manias and of the virtues which were later to go into the make-up of Bramble. Here was the armature of my character, a certain way of thinking, of feeling. Most of the traits, however, which were later to make up the Bramble of the book did not derive from this man, but from other colonels who came to visit us, from generals under whom I was later to serve, in fact from a good twenty different models.

Now here is, I think, the clearest way to explain how this work took shape. There were various officers living in our mess who corresponded to different types of Britons. There was the colonel who represented 'a Bramble direction', the strong, silent type; there was a brilliant and paradoxical major who played the role of the Tory Englishman, the die-hard, proud of his prejudices; there was a psychiatrist with a sarcastic turn of mind out of whom I was to fashion Dr O'Grady; there was a Scottish padre whom I depicted very accurately; and then there was a Frenchman, myself, who wrote letters in verse to the considerable scandal of the colonel, and whom I turned into the interpreter Aurelle.

In order to bring one's characters to life, however, simply finding the models is not enough; it still remains

[8]

to withdraw from them and free oneself of them. Fate now provided me with the opportunity. In 1916 I had a heart attack and the doctors 'evacuated' me. After convalescence I was sent to Abbeville and attached to a headquarters staff. Here, much to my surprise, I ran into the officers from my earlier mess, under other names. It now came home to me that if the Englishman in abstract does not exist, certain boldly defined individuals can convey his essence.

Here, then, resides the mystery of Bramble. Bramble, born of a hotchpotch of colonels, became more real for me than any colonel. I soon knew, by a secret instinct, what Bramble would have said, what he would have thought on any subject. My greatest joy came the day when, having put some words into the colonel's mouth to conclude a story (the one about the woman who gets herself pregnant by the most handsome of the officers), I heard my English friends assure me that this reflexion was 'the most Bramble of all'.

This book had the good fortune to be elaborated slowly. The war gave me leisure to let my thoughts simmer. For a long time I thought I would have to write a traditional novel with a plot, love, adventures. Then I had the idea of this book of conversations, a book of ideas, a metaphysical novel, to use the current expression. For *Bramble*, despite its tone which is humorous, is essentially a philosophical novel in which the materialistic determinism of Dr O'Grady is opposed to the padre's religion and the silent faith of the colonel. It is also a study of the British character. I loved the men among whom I was living and I had attempted to describe their virtues.

In 1917 the book was finished, but how to have it

A*   [9]

published? I knew no one in the publishing world and besides, I was with the army, far from Paris. A French comrade, Captain de Mun, read my manuscript and told me:

'It's original and amusing. Furthermore, the book can improve Franco-British relations; it must be published.'

I replied that this was impossible for I knew no publishers. He shook with laughter.

'But publishers are not unapproachable monsters,' he said. 'They're men whose job it is to read everything. On Monday I'm going to Paris on leave. I shall give your manuscript to quite a young publisher, Bernard Grasset—he's published the first works of Giraudoux . . .'

In short, this daring captain took my manuscript, and a few weeks later Grasset wrote me a cordial letter. He had decided to publish the book. A few months later we were before Amiens, and the enemy had just broken through our front, when I received the first copies. 'Send them,' Grasset told me, 'with a dedication, to the critics you know.' I knew no critics and decided to offer them to men I admired: Clémenceau, Anatole France, Kipling. They all replied, very kindly, inviting me to visit them after the war.

Then came the reviews. What joy and delight for a beginner: they were all excellent! I was later to realize that there are two moments in the career of letters when you are read with kindness: first, when the critics can discover you and then when you are about to disappear from the scene. Add that I was an officer, in time of war—this was a good card in my hand. Meanwhile letters arrived from Paris, from Grasset: 'It's selling splendidly.' His first printing had been three thousand copies. These sold out in a week. Five thousand more were run off. All sold. And so it went on: ten thousand, thirty thousand, fifty thousand. I was amazed—and delighted.

My friend Major Wake had his sister, Thurfrida Wake, translate *Bramble*; she suggested it to John Lane of The Bodley Head. Thus it was that I entered into contact—and into friendship—with my first British publisher. Those English readers who had a sense of humour—that is to say nearly all—were amused by this little opus which drew a sympathetic portrait of them. The others said:

'Why the devil has this damned Frenchman gone and put down conversations which absolutely anyone might have? It doesn't contain a single sentence I don't come out with myself every night in the mess.'

The criticism enchanted me, it was so very Bramble. As for the genuine Colonel Brambles, my models, they did not read it, of course. They read only the *Times*, the *Army List* and the occasional thriller. There were, nonetheless, a few English generals sufficiently 'un-Bramble' to read my book and even to tell me so. After the war Lord Byng of Vimy offered me a dinner at the Atheneum to which he had invited, so he told me, samples of every type of Englishman.

'You'll change neighbour after each course,' said Lord Byng, 'and at the end of the meal you'll know England.'

At the dessert he spoke up. 'Messiou,' said he, 'we are all Bramble here.'

A writer's greatest boast is that of having created a type. This has, alas, not often fallen to me, but I think that Bramble has, to some extent, had a life of his own outside the pages of my book and, since the Bodley Head have seen fit to reissue it in a new edition, I hope that he will survive me. Perhaps he will kill me, for he has already done so once.

It was during the war, in 1940. I had enlisted and was once more attached to the British army. I was asked to go to England (before the German offensive in May) to speak to the cadets at a flying school. I gave a talk in English, as best I could, to a few hundred young pilots in light blue uniform. As I left the hall I was engulfed in the flood of cadets, and I overheard one of them, who was walking behind me and therefore could not recognize me, ask his neighbour:

'Who's the old boy who's just been talking to us?'

'I don't know,' replied the other. 'It seems he's some colonel called Bramble.'

The creature had thus taken the place of the creator, something which, I admit, fills the creator with joy.

As for Dr O'Grady (who in real life was called Dr James), I have often seen him since—in particular when I wrote the life of Sir Alexander Fleming. I asked Lady Fleming if I could meet some doctors who had been students with Fleming.

'There is Dr James,' she said.

'That cannot be *my* James,' I said. 'It would be too marvellous.'

But it was indeed *my* James: it was Dr O'Grady in person. He came to see me in Périgord. As I awaited him on the station platform at Limoges, I wondered: 'Are we going to recognize each other in this crowd after so many years?' All at once I saw my friend. There could be no doubt: grey at the temples, true enough; in place of the khaki uniform, the dark overcoat which befitted a great English doctor; but the same smile, ironic and affectionate.

We effortlessly slipped back into the tone of the conversations we used to have. The body ages, the mind is eternal, and our friendship was founded on ideas. We took walks in the country with the same rapid stride as when we used to walk to Ypres across the hop and beetroot fields of Flanders.

'This country can have changed very little,' he observed, 'since the time when the Roman legionaries were stationed here and complained at being kept far from Rome and their wives by a damned colonial war.'

I looked at him, delighted; I had rediscovered exactly the Dr O'Grady I remembered. The man and the character coincided. And once more I was captivated, as I always am, by this inimitable charm of the best Englishmen, which is compounded of straightforwardness, simplicity and humour.

February, 1965   ANDRÉ MAUROIS

THE SILENCE OF
COLONEL BRAMBLE

*Translated from the French
by Thurfrida Wake
Verses translated
by Wilfrid Jackson*

In Memoriam
J. A.–M.

CONTENTS

I The True Sporting Spirit, 19

II Military Correspondence, 23

III Dr O'Grady on Revolutions, 28

IV Aurelle's Letter, 35

V Rain, 40

VI Hunters' Tales, 45

VII Poetry is Rhymed Foolishness, 51

VIII 0275 Private Scott, 57

IX On Padres and Padres, 61

X Award for Valour, 65

XI The Brigade and the Village, 69

XII The Captain and the Masked Lady, 75

XIII A Poem, 83

XIV Extracts from Aurelle's Diary, 85

XV A Great Attack, 90

XVI Chanson du Comte de Dorset, 98

XVII Ants in Khaki, 100

XVIII 'Transmitted to the Proper Quarter', 104

XIX A Miraculous Cure, 110

XX A Pause in the Conversation, 116

XXI Long Live Whoever-it-is!, 123

XXII Another Poem, 129

XXIII To do with Goats, 130

XXIV Crécy Revisited, 136

Appendix The Verse in the Original, 145

CHAPTER I

THE TRUE SPORTING SPIRIT

The Highland Brigade was holding its regimental boxing match in a fine old Flemish barn in the neighbourhood of Poperinghe. At the end of the evening the general got on to a chair and, in a clear, audible voice, said:

'Gentlemen, we have today seen some excellent fighting, from which I think we may learn some useful lessons for the more important contest that we shall shortly resume; we must keep our heads, we must keep our eyes open, we must hit seldom but hit hard, and we must fight to a finish.'

Three cheers made the old barn shake. The motors purred at the door. Colonel Bramble, Major Parker and the French interpreter, Aurelle, went on foot to their billets among the hop and beetroot fields.

'We are a curious nation,' said Major Parker. 'To interest a Frenchman in a boxing match you must tell him that his national honour is at stake. To interest an Englishman in a war you need only suggest that it is a kind of a boxing match. Tell us that the Hun is a barbarian, we agree politely, but tell us that he is a bad sportsman and you rouse the British Empire.'

'It is the Hun's fault,' said the colonel sadly, 'that war is no longer a gentleman's game.'

'We never imagined,' continued the major, 'that such cads existed. Bombing open towns is nearly as unpardonable as fishing for trout with a worm, or shooting a fox.'

'You must not exaggerate, Parker,' said the colonel calmly. 'They are not as bad as that yet.'

Then he asked Aurelle politely if the boxing had amused him.

'I particularly admired, sir, the sporting discipline of your men. During the boxing the Highlanders behaved as if they were in church.'

'The true sporting spirit has always something religious about it,' said the major. 'A few years ago when the New Zealand football team visited England, and from the first match beat the English teams, the country was as upset as if we had lost this war. Every one in the streets and trains went about with long faces. Then the New Zealanders beat Scotland, then Ireland; the end of the world had come! However, there remained the Welsh. On the day of the match there were one hundred thousand persons on the ground. You know that the Welsh are deeply religious and that their national anthem, "Land of our Fathers", is also a prayer. When the two teams arrived the whole crowd, men and women, exalted and confident, sang this hymn to God before the battle, and the New Zealanders were beaten. Ah, we are a great nation!'

'Indeed, yes,' said Aurelle, quite overcome, 'you are a great nation.' He added, after a moment's silence, 'But you were also quite right just now when you said you were a curious nation in some things, and your opinion of people astonishes us sometimes. You say, "Brown looks an idiot, but he's not, he played cricket for Essex." Or, "At Eton we took him for a fool, but at Oxford he surprised us. Do you know he is plus four at golf, and won the high jump?"'

'Well?' said the colonel.

'Don't you think, sir, that cleverness——'

'I hate clever people—— Oh, I beg your pardon, messiou.'

'That's very kind of you, sir,' said Aurelle.

'Glad you take it like that,' growled the colonel into his moustache.

He spoke seldom and always in short sentences, but Aurelle had learnt to appreciate his dry and vigorous humour and the charming smile which often lit up his rugged countenance.

'But don't you find yourself, Aurelle,' went on Major Parker, 'that intelligence is over-estimated with you? It is certainly more useful to know how to box than how to write. You would like Eton to go in for nothing but learning? It is just like asking a trainer of racehorses to be interested in circus horses. We don't go to school to learn, but to be soaked in the prejudices of our class, without which we should be useless and unhappy. We are like the young Persians Herodotus talks about, who up to the age of twenty only learnt three sciences: to ride, to shoot and to tell the truth.'

'That may be,' said Aurelle, 'but just see, major, how inconsistent you are. You despise learning and you quote Herodotus. Better still, I caught you the other day in the act of reading a translation of Xenophon in your dug-out. Very few Frenchmen, I assure you——'

'That's quite different,' said the major. 'The Greeks and Romans interest us, not as objects of study, but as ancestors and sportsmen. We are the direct heirs of the mode of life of the Greeks and of the Roman Empire. Xenophon amuses me because he is a perfect type of the English gentleman, with his hunting and fishing stories, and descriptions of battles. When I read in Cicero: "Scandal in the Colonial Office. Grave accusations against Sir Marcus Varro, Governor-General of Sicily," you can well understand that that sounds to me like old family history. And who was your Alcibiades, pray, but a Winston Churchill, without the hats ?'

The scenery round them was very picturesque: the Mont des Cats, the Mont Rouge, and the Mont Noir made a framework for the heavy, motionless clouds of an old Dutch painting. The peasants' houses with their weather-beaten, thatched roofs faded into the surrounding fields; their dull walls had turned the colour of yellow clay. The grey shutters bordered with green struck the only vivid and human note in this kingdom of the earth.

The colonel pointed with his cane to a new mine crater; but Major Parker, sticking to his point, went on with his favourite subject:

'The greatest service which sport has rendered us is that it has saved us from intellectual culture. Luckily one hasn't time for everything, and golf and tennis cut out reading. We are stupid——'

'Nonsense, major!' said Aurelle.

'We are stupid,' emphatically repeated Major Parker, who hated being contradicted, 'and it is a great asset. When we are in danger we don't notice it, because we don't reflect; so we keep cool and come out of it nearly always with honour.'

'Always,' amended Colonel Bramble with his Scotch curtness.

And Aurelle, hopping agilely over the enormous ruts by the side of these two Goliaths, realized more clearly than ever that this war would end well.

CHAPTER II

MILITARY CORRESPONDENCE

'Clear the table,' said Colonel Bramble to the orderlies. 'Bring the rum, a lemon, some sugar and hot water, and keep some more boiling. Then tell my batman to give me the gramophone and the box of records.'

This gramophone, a gift to the Highlanders from a very patriotic old lady, was the colonel's pride. He had it carried about after him everywhere and treated it with delicate care, feeding it every month with fresh records.

'Messiou,' he said to Aurelle, 'what would you like, "The Bing Boys", "Destiny Waltz", or "Caruso"?'

Major Parker and Dr O'Grady solemnly consigned Edison and all his works to a hotter place; the padre raised his eyes to heaven.

'Anything you like, sir,' said Aurelle, 'except "Caruso".'

'Why?' said the colonel. 'It's a very good record, it cost twenty-two shillings. But first of all you must hear my dear Mrs Finzi-Magrini in "La Tosca". Doctor, please regulate it, I can't see very well—Speed 61. Don't scratch the record, for God's sake!'

He sank down on his biscuit boxes, arranged his back comfortably against a heap of sacks, and shut his eyes. His rugged face relaxed. The padre and the doctor were playing chess, and Major Parker was filling in long returns for brigade headquarters. Over a little wood, torn to bits by shells, an aeroplane was sailing home among fleecy white clouds in a lovely pale-green sky. Aurelle began a letter.

'Padre,' said the doctor, 'if you are going to the division tomorrow, ask them to send me some blankets for our dead Boches. You saw the one we buried this morning? The rats had half eaten him. It's indecent. Check to the king.'

'Yes,' said the padre, 'and it's curious how they always begin at the nose!'

Over their heads a heavy English battery began to bombard the German line. The padre smiled broadly.

'There'll be dirty work at the cross roads tonight,' he remarked with satisfaction.

'Padre,' said the doctor, 'are you not the minister of a religion of peace and love?'

'The Master said, my boy, that one must love one's fellow-man. He never said that we must love Germans. I take your knight.'

The Reverend John MacIvor, an old military chaplain, with a face bronzed by Eastern suns, took to this life of war and horrors with the enthusiasm of a child. When the men were in the trenches he visited them every morning with his pockets bulging with hymn-books and packets of cigarettes. While resting behind the lines, he tried his hand at bombing and deplored the fact that his cloth forbade him human targets.

Major Parker suddenly stopped his work to curse Brass Hats and their absurd questions.

'When I was in the Himalayas at Chitral,' he said, 'some red-hats sent us a ridiculous scheme for manoeuvres; among other details the artillery had to cross a rocky defile hardly wide enough for a very thin man.

'I wired, "Scheme received; send immediately a hundred barrels of vinegar." "Report yourself to the P.M.O. for mental examination," courteously remarked headquarters. "Re-read 'Hannibal's Campaign'," I replied.'

'You really sent that telegram?' asked Aurelle. 'In the French army you would have been court-martialled.'

'That's because our two nations have not the same idea of liberty,' said the major. 'To us the inalienable rights of man are humour, sport, and primogeniture.'

'At the headquarters of the brigade,' said the padre, 'there is a captain who must have had lessons from you in military correspondence. The other day, as I had no news of one of my young chaplains who had left us about a month, I sent a note to the brigade: "The Reverend C. Carlisle was invalided on September 12th. I should like to know if he is better, and if he has been given a new appointment." The reply from the hospital said simply: "1. Condition unchanged. 2. Ultimate destination unknown." The officer in transmitting it to me had added, "It is not clear whether the last paragraph refers to the unit to which the Rev C. Carlisle will be eventually attached, or to his eternal welfare." '

The Italian air came to an end with a triumphant roulade.

'What a voice!' said the colonel, opening his eyes regretfully.

He carefully stopped the record and put it affectionately in its case.

'Now, messiou, I am going to play "Destiny Waltz." '

One could just see outside the Verey lights gently rising and falling. The padre and the doctor went on describing their corpses while carefully manoeuvring the ivory pieces of the little set of chessmen; the howitzers and machine-guns broke into the voluptuous rhythm of the waltz, creating a sort of fantastic symphony highly appreciated by Aurelle. He continued to write his letter in easy verses.

> '*Death is a-foot; Fate calls the tune;*
>   *Lose not a minute—*
> *Forget ! But wear your black till—June;*
>   *You're charming in it.*
>
> *I will not have you come with tears,*
>   *With roses vain;*
> *Young life will ask, in coming years,*
>   *Your rose again.*

'Don't be angry with me, dearest, if I descend to the lowest level of "romantics": a clergyman and a doctor, beside me, are intent on playing the role of the Grave-diggers in *Hamlet*.

> '*Pity me not, for I shall sleep*
>   *Like any child,*
> *And from my changing earth up leap*
>   *The grasses wild.*
>
> *But if, when summer hours grow few,*
>   *And dusk is long,*
> *Your gaze, madonna-calm, should do*
>   *Your beauty wrong,*
>
> *Nor lend that sadness to your face*
>   *I cherish yet,*
> *Forget then, for a little space,*
>   *That you forget.*'

'Do you like my waltz, messiou?' said the colonel.

'Very much indeed, sir,' said Aurelle sincerely.

The colonel gave him a grateful smile.

'I'll play it again for you, messiou. Doctor, regulate the gramophone slower, speed 59. Don't scratch the record. For *you*, this time, messiou.'

CHAPTER III

DR O'GRADY ON REVOLUTIONS

BOSWELL. 'Why then, sir, did he talk so?'
JOHNSON. 'Why, sir, to make you answer as you did.'

The batteries were asleep; Major Parker was answering questions from the brigade; the orderlies brought the rum, sugar and boiling water; the colonel put the gramophone to speed 61, and Dr O'Grady talked about the Russian Revolution.

'It is unprecedented,' said he, 'for the men who made a revolution to remain in power after it is over. Yet one still finds revolutionaries: that proves how badly history is taught.'

'Parker,' said the colonel, 'pass the port.'

'Ambition,' said Aurelle, 'is after all not the only motive that inspires men to action. One can be a revolutionary from hatred of a tyrant, from jealousy, or even from the love of humanity.'

Major Parker abandoned his papers.

'I admire France very much, Aurelle, especially since this war; but one thing shocks me in your country, if you will allow me to speak plainly, and that is your jealousy of equality. When I read the history of your Revolution I am sorry I was not there to kick Robespierre and that horrible fellow Hébert. And your *sans-culottes*. Well, that makes me long to dress up in purple satin and gold lace and walk about the Place de la Concorde.'

The doctor allowed a particularly acute attack of hysteria on the part of Madame Finzi-Magrini to pass, and went on:

'The love of humanity is a pathological state of a sexual origin which often appears at the age of puberty in nervous and clever people. The excess of phosphorus in the system must get out somewhere. As for hatred of a tyrant, that is a more human sentiment which has full play in time of war, when force and the mob are one. Emperors must be mad fools to decide on declaring wars which substitute an armed nation for their Prætorian Guards. That idiocy accomplished, despotism of course produces revolution until terrorism leads to the inevitable reaction.'

'You condemn us then, doctor, to oscillate between rebellion and a *coup d'état*?'

'No,' said the doctor, 'because the English people, who have already given the world Stilton cheese and comfortable chairs, have invented for our benefit the Parliamentary system. Our M.P.'s arrange rebellions and *coups d'état* for us, which leaves the rest of the nation time to play cricket. The Press completes the system by enabling us to take our share in these tumults by proxy. All these things form a part of modern comfort and in a hundred years' time every man, white, yellow, red or black, will refuse to inhabit a room without hot water laid on, or a country without a Parliament.'

'I hope you are wrong,' said Major Parker. 'I hate politicians, and I want after the War, to go and live in the East, because nobody out there pays any attention to a government of babblers.'

'My dear major, why the devil do you mix your personal feelings with these questions? Politics are controlled by laws as necessary as the movements of the stars. Are you annoyed that there are dark nights because you happen to prefer moonlight? Humanity lies on an uncomfortable bed. When the sleeper aches too much he turns over, that is a war or an insurrection. Then he goes to sleep again for a few centuries. All that is quite natural and happens without much suffering, if one does not mix up any moral ideas with it. Attacks of cramp are not virtues. But each change finds, alas, its prophets who, from the love of humanity, as Aurelle says, put this miserable globe to fire and sword.'

'That's very well said, doctor,' said Aurelle, 'but I return the compliment; if those are your sentiments, why do you take the trouble to belong to a party? Because you are a damned socialist.'

'Doctor,' said the colonel, 'pass the port.'

'Ah,' said the doctor, 'that's because I would rather be persecutor than persecuted. You must know how to recognize the arrival of these periodical upheavals and prepare. This war will bring socialism, that is to say, the total sacrifice of the aristocrat to the Leviathan. This in itself is neither a blessing nor a misfortune: it is cramp. Let us then turn over with a good grace, as long as we feel we shall be more comfortable on the other side.'

'That's a perfectly absurd theory,' said Major Parker, angrily sticking out his square chin, 'and if you adopt it, doctor, you must give up medicine! Why try and stop the course of diseases? They are also, according to you, periodic and necessary upheavals. But if you pretend to fight against tuberculosis do not deny me the right to attack universal suffrage.'

At this moment a R.A.M.C. sergeant entered and

asked Dr O'Grady to come and see a wounded man: Major Parker remained master of the situation. The colonel, who had a horror of arguments, seized the opportunity to talk about something else.

'Messiou,' he said, 'what is the displacement of one of your largest cruisers?'

'Sixty thousand tons, sir,' hazarded Aurelle wildly.

This knock-out blow put the colonel out of action, and Aurelle asked Major Parker why he objected to universal suffrage.

'But don't you see, my dear Aurelle, that it is the most extravagant idea that humanity has ever conceived? Our political system will be considered more monstrous than slavery in a thousand years. One man, one vote, whatever the man is! Do you pay the same price for a good horse as for a crock?'

'Have you ever heard the immortal reasoning of our Courteline? "Why should I pay twelve francs for an umbrella when I can get a glass of beer for six sous?"'

'Equal rights for men!' continued the major vehemently. 'Why not equal courage and equal intelligence while you are about it?'

Aurelle loved the major's impassioned and pleasant harangues and, to keep the discussion going, said that he did not see how one could refuse a people the right to choose their leaders.

'To control them, Aurelle, yes; but to choose them, never! An aristocracy cannot be elected. It is or it isn't. Why, if I were to attempt to choose the Commander-in-Chief or the Superintendent of Guy's Hospital I should be shut up; but, if I wish to have a voice in the election of the Chancellor of the Exchequer or the First Lord of the Admiralty, I'm a good citizen!'

'That is not quite correct, major. Ministers are not elected. Mind, I agree with you that our political system is imperfect; but so are all human affairs. And then, '*La pire des Chambres vaut mieux que la meilleure des antichambres.*" '

'I piloted round London lately,' replied the major, 'an Arab chief who honoured me with his friendship, and when I had shown him the House of Commons and explained what went on there, he remarked :"It must give you a lot of trouble cutting off those six hundred heads when you are not pleased with the Government." '

'Messiou,' said the colonel, exasperated, 'I am going to play "Destiny Waltz" for you.'

.　　　.　　　.

Major Parker remained silent while the waltz unrolled its rhythmic phrases, but he ruminated over his old resentment against that 'horrible fellow Hébert' and, as soon as the record had ground out its final notes, he started a new attack on Aurelle.

'What advantage,' he said, 'could the French have found in changing their government eight times in a century ? Revolutions have become a national institution with you. In England, it would be impossible. If a crowd collected at Westminster and made a disturbance, the policeman would tell them to go away and they would do so.'

'What an idea!' said Aurelle, who did not like Revolutions, but who thought he ought to defend an old French lady against this hot-headed Saxon. 'You must not forget, major, that you also cut off your King's head. No policeman intervened to save Charles Stuart, as far as I know.'

'The assassination of Charles I,' said the major, 'was the sole work of Oliver Cromwell; now Oliver was a very good cavalry colonel, but he knew nothing of the real feelings of the English people, which they showed pretty plainly at the time of the Restoration.

'Cromwell's head, which had been embalmed, was stuck on a pike on the top of Westminster Hall. One stormy night the wind broke the shaft of the pike and the head rolled to the feet of a sentry. He took it home and hid it in the chimney of his house, where it remained until his death. It passed through various hands till it came into the possession of a friend of mine, and I have often sat at tea opposite the head of the Protector still on its broken pike. One could easily recognize the wart which he had on his forehead and there still remains a lock of chestnut hair.'

'Humph,' grunted the colonel, at last interested in the conversation.

'Besides,' continued the major, 'the English Revolution does not compare in any way with the French one: it did not weaken the ruling classes. As a matter of fact, all the bad business of 1789 was caused by Louis XIV. Instead of leaving your country the strong armour of a landed gentry he made his nobles into the ridiculous puppets of Versailles, whose sole business was to hand him his coat and his waistcoat. In destroying the prestige of a class which should be the natural supporters of the monarchy, he ruined it beyond repair, and more's the pity.'

'It is very easy for you to criticize us,' said Aurelle. 'We made our Revolution for you; the most important

B   [33]

event in English history is the taking of the Bastille, and well you know it.'

'Bravo, messiou,' said the colonel, 'stick up for your country. One ought always to stick up for one's country. Now please pass the port. I am going to play you "The Mikado".'

CHAPTER IV

AURELLE'S LETTER

Somewhere in France

Singing, the soldiers go their way:
'Stow your troubles inside your kit.'
Such rain and wind, that you'd rather stay
Indoors, than walk out with your girl in it.
Singing, the soldiers go their way:
I'm making you verses so here I sit;
Singing, the soldiers go their way:
'Stow your troubles inside your kit.'

Here is the orderly bringing, let's say,
Last week's papers, perhaps a chit;
Stale chatter of old political play,
'Stow your troubles inside your kit.'
All we can do, though the year is at May,
Best we can furnish by way of wit;
Singing, the soldiers go their way:
'Stow your troubles inside your kit.'

Rain on the window, beating like spray,
Storms an accompaniment, noisily fit,
To some prelude of Wagner's forgotten day,
'Stow your troubles inside your kit.'
Who knows but tomorrow a howitzer may

Give me uncivil notice to quit?
But Satan may ask me to wet my clay—
So 'Stow your troubles inside your kit':
Singing, the soldiers go their way.

Grey dawn is breaking over the spongy plain. Today will be the same as yesterday, tomorrow like today. The doctor will wave his arms and say, 'Très triste, messiou,' and he will not know what is sad, no more shall I. Then he will give me a humorous lecture in a style between Bernard Shaw and the Bible.

The padre will write letters, play patience and go out riding. The guns will thunder, Boches will be killed, some of our men too. We shall lunch off bully beef and boiled potatoes, the beer will be horrible and the colonel will say to me, 'Bière française no bonne, messiou.'

In the evening, after a dinner of badly cooked mutton, with mint sauce, and boiled potatoes, the inevitable gramophone will appear. We shall have 'The Arcadians', 'The Mikado', then 'Destiny Waltz'—'pour vous messiou' —and 'Mrs Finzi-Magrini' for the colonel, and finally 'The Lancashire Ramble'. Unfortunately for me, the first time I heard this circus tune I imitated a juggler catching balls in time to the music. This little comedy henceforth took its place in the traditions of the Mess, and if this evening at the first notes of the 'Ramble' I should forget to play my part the colonel will say, 'Allons, messiou, allons,' pretending to juggle, but I know my duty and I shall not forget; for Colonel Bramble only cares for familiar scenes and fine old crusted jokes.

His favourite number is a recitation by O'Grady of 'Going on leave.' When he is in a bad temper, when one of his old friends has been made a brigadier-general, or been given a C.B., this recitation is the only thing that can make him smile. He knows it by heart and, like the children, stops the doctor if he misses a sentence or alters a reply.

'No, doctor, no; the Naval officer said to you, "When you hear four loud short whistles, it means that the ship has been torpedoed," and you replied, "And what if the torpedo carries away the whistle?"'

The doctor, having found his place, goes on.

Parker, too, one day found a remark which ever afterwards had a brilliant success. He got it out of a letter that a chaplain had written to the *Times*. 'The life of the soldier,' wrote this excellent man, 'is one of great hardship; not infrequently mingled with moments of real danger.'

The colonel thoroughly enjoys the unconscious humour of this remark, and would quote it whenever a shell scattered gravel over him. But his great resource, if the conversation bores him, is to attack the padre on his two weak points: bishops and Scotsmen.

The padre, who comes from the Highlands, is madly patriotic. He is convinced that it is only the Scots who play the game and who are really killed.

'If history told the truth,' he says, 'this war would not be called the European War, but the war between Scotland and Germany.'

The colonel is Scotch himself, but he is fair, and every time he finds in the papers the casualty lists of the Irish Guards or the Welsh Fusiliers he reads them out in a loud voice to the padre, who, to keep his end up, maintains that the Welsh Fusiliers and Irish Guards are recruited in Aberdeen. This is his invariable retort.

All this may appear rather puerile to you, my friend,

but these childish things are the only bright spots in our boring, bombarded existence. Yes, these wonderful men have remained children in many ways; they have the fresh outlook, and the inordinate love of games, and our rustic shelter often seems to me like a nursery of heroes.

But I have profound faith in them; their profession of empire-builders has inspired them with high ideals of the duty of the white man. The colonel and Parker are 'Sahibs' whom nothing on earth would turn from the path they have chosen. To despise danger, to stand firm under fire, is not an act of courage in their eyes—it is simply part of their education. If a small dog stands up to a big one they say gravely, 'He is a gentleman.'

A true gentleman, you see, is very nearly the most sympathetic type which evolution has produced among the pitiful group of creatures who are at this moment making such a noise in the world. Amid the horrible wickedness of the species, the English have established an oasis of courtesy and phlegm. I love them.

I must add that it is a very foolish error to imagine that they are less intelligent than ourselves, in spite of the delight my friend Major Parker pretends to take in affirming the contrary. The truth is that their intelligence follows a different method from ours. Far removed from our standard of rationalism and the pedantic sentiment of the Germans, they delight in a vigorous common sense and all absence of system. Hence a natural and simple manner which makes their sense of humour still more delightful.

But I see, from my window, my horse waiting for me; and I must go round to the surly farmers and get some straw for the quartermaster, who is trying to build stables. But *you* are furnishing boudoirs, and mind you choose, O Amazon, soft, oriental silks.

> *In your salon, style 'Directory'*
> *(Lavender-blue and lemon-yellow)*
> *Ancient armchairs sit, hail-fellow,*
> *In a fashion contradictory,*
> *With a sofa lacking history*
> *(Lavender-blue and lemon-yellow).*
>
> *To our Merveilleuses notorious*
> *(Lavender-blue and lemon-yellow)*
> *Dandies striped with chevrons mellow*
> *Shall proclaim a day victorious,*
> *Decked in dolmans all-vainglorious*
> *(Lavender-blue and lemon-yellow).*
>
> *Walls severe, as bare as a church,*
> *(Lavender-blue and lemon-yellow)*
> *May wait awhile the brutal bellow*
> *Of some First-Consul, who may lurch*
> *Upon their calm of days memorial*
> *With his visage dictatorial*
> *(Lavender eyed, and skin of yellow).*

'Are you a poet?' the colonel asked me doubtfully, when he saw me writing lines of equal length.

I denied the soft impeachment.

CHAPTER V

RAIN

It had been raining for four days. The heavy raindrops played a monotonous tattoo on the curved roof of the tent. Outside in the field the grass had disappeared under yellow mud, in which the men's footsteps sounded like the smacking of a giant's lips.

' "And God looked upon the earth, and behold, it was corrupt," ' recited the padre; ' "and God said to Noah, Make thee an ark of gopher wood; rooms shalt thou make in the ark, and shalt pitch it within and without with pitch. The same day were all the fountains of the great deep broken up, and the windows of heaven were opened," ' continued the doctor.

'The Flood,' he added, 'was a real event, for its description is common to all oriental mythology. No doubt the Euphrates had burst its banks; that's why the Ark was driven into the interior and came to rest on a hill. Similar catastrophes often occur in Mesopotamia and in India, but are rare in Belgium.'

'The cyclone of 1876 killed 215,000 people in Bengal,' said the colonel. 'Messiou, send round the port, please.'

The colonel loved statistics, to the great misfortune of Aurelle, who, quite incapable of remembering figures, was interrogated every day on the number of inhabitants in a village, the strength of the Serbian army, or the initial velocity of the French bullet. He foresaw with terror that the colonel was going to ask him the average depth of rain in feet and inches in Flanders, and he hastened to create a diversion.

'I found in Poperinghe,' he said, showing the book he was reading, 'this very curious old volume. It is a description of England and Scotland by the Frenchman, Etienne Perlin, Paris, 1558.'

'Humph! What does this Mr Perlin say?' asked the colonel, who had the same respect for ancient things as he had for old soldiers.

Aurelle opened the book at hazard and translated:

' "After dinner, the cloth is withdrawn and the ladies retire. The table is of beautiful glossy Indian wood, and stands of the same wood hold the bottles. The name of each wine is engraved on a silver plate which hangs by a little chain round the neck of the bottle. The guests each choose the wine they like and drink it as seriously as if they were doing penance, while proposing the health of eminent personages or the fashionable beauties; this is what is known as a toast." '

'I like "fashionable beauties",' said the doctor. 'Perhaps Aurelle will take to drinking port, now he can pour libations to Gaby Deslys or Gladys Cooper.'

'There are toasts for each day in the week,' said the colonel, 'Monday, our men; Tuesday, ourselves; Wednesday, our swords; Thursday, sport; Friday, our religion; Saturday, sweethearts and wives; Sunday, absent friends and ships at sea.'

Aurelle went on reading aloud:

' "These toasts are of barbaric origin, and I have been told that the Highlanders of Scotland, a semi-savage folk who live in a state of perpetual feud——" '

'Listen to that, padre,' said the colonel. 'Read it again,

messiou, for the padre. "I have been told that the Highlanders of Scotland——" '

' "A semi-savage folk who live in a state of perpetual feud, have kept to the original character of this custom. To drink the health of anyone is to ask him to guard you while you drink and cannot defend yourself; and the person to whom you drink replies, 'I pledge you,' which means in their language, 'I guarantee your safety.' Then he draws his dagger, places the point on the table and protects you until your glass is empty." '

'That's why,' said Major Parker, 'the pewter pots that they give for golf prizes have always got glass bottoms through which one can see the dagger of the assassin.'

'Send round the port, messiou, I want to drink the padre's health in a second glass to hear him reply, "I pledge you," and to see him put the point of his dagger on the table.'

'I've only got a Swiss knife,' said the padre.

'That's good enough,' said the colonel.

'This theory of the origin of toasts is very probable,' said the doctor. 'We are always repeating ancestral signs which are quite useless now. When a great actress wants to express hate she draws back her charming lips and shows her canine teeth, an unconscious sign of cannibalism. We shake hands with a friend to prevent him using it to strike us, and we take off our hats because our ancestors used to humbly offer their heads, to the bigwigs of those days, to be cut off.'

At that moment there was a loud crack, and Colonel Bramble fell backwards with a crash. One of the legs of his chair had broken. The doctor and Parker helped him up, while Aurelle and the padre looked on in fits of laughter.

'There's a good example of an ancestral survival,"
said the major, kindly intervening to save Aurelle, who
was trying in vain to stop laughing. 'I imagine that one
laughs at a fall because the death of a man was one of
the most amusing sights for our ancestors. It delivered
them from an adversary and diminished the number of
those who shared the food and the females.'

'Now we know you, messiou,' said the colonel.

'A French philosopher,' said Aurelle, who had by
this time recovered, 'has constructed quite a different
theory of laughter: he is called Bergson and——'

'I have heard of him,' said the padre; 'he's a clergyman, isn't he?'

'I have a theory about laughter,' said the doctor,
'which is more edifying than yours, major. I think it is
simply produced by a feeling of horror, immediately
succeeded by a feeling of relief. A young monkey who is
devoted to the old father of the tribe sees him slip on
a banana skin, he fears an accident and his chest swells
with fright, then he discovers that it's nothing and all
his muscles pleasantly relax. That was the first joke, and
it explains the convulsive motions in laughing. Aurelle
is shaken physically because he is shaken morally by
two strong motives: his anxious affection and respect for
the colonel——'

'Ugh,' grunted the colonel.

'And the consoling certainty that he is not hurt.'

'I wish you would talk about something else,' said the
colonel. 'Read a little more of the book, messiou.'

Aurelle turned over some pages.

' "Other nations," ' he read, ' "accuse the English of
incivility because they arrive and depart without touch-
ing their hats, and without that flow of compliments

which are common to the French and Italians. But those who judge thus see things in a false light. The English idea is that politeness does not consist in gestures or words which are often hypocritical and deceptive, but in being courteously disposed to other people. They have their faults like every nation, but, considering everything, I am sure that the more one knows them the more one esteems and likes them." '

'I like old Mr Perlin,' said the colonel. 'Do you agree with him, messiou ?'

'The whole of France now agrees with him, sir,' said Aurelle warmly.

'You are biased, Aurelle,' said Major Parker, 'because you are getting quite English yourself. You whistle in your bath, you drink whisky and are beginning to like arguments; if you could only manage to eat tomatoes and underdone cutlets for breakfast you would be perfect.'

'If you don't mind, major, I would rather remain French,' said Aurelle. 'Besides, I never knew that whistling in one's bath was an English rite.'

'So much so,' said the doctor, 'that I have arranged to have carved on my tombstone: "Here lies a British subject who never whistled in his bath or tried to be an amateur detective." '

CHAPTER VI

HUNTERS' TALES

British conversation is like a game of cricket or a boxing match; personal allusions are forbidden like hitting below the belt, and anyone who loses his temper is disqualified.

Aurelle met at the Lennox Mess veterinaries and generals, tradesmen and dukes. Excellent whisky was provided and the guests entertained in a friendly way without boring them with too much attention.

'It rains a lot in your country,' said a major in the Engineers who sat next to him one evening.

'So it does in England,' said Aurelle.

'I intend,' said the major, 'when this damned war is over, to leave the army and go and live in New Zealand.'

'You have friends there?'

'Oh, no, but the salmon fishing is very good.'

'Bring your rod over here while we are resting, major, the pond is full of enormous pike.'

'I never fish for pike,' said the major, 'he is not a gentleman. When he sees he is caught he gives up; the salmon fights to the end, even without hope. A thirty-pound fellow will sometimes fight two hours; that's something like, isn't it?'

'Admirable!' said Aurelle. 'And what about trout?'

'The trout is a lady,' said the major; 'you must deceive her; but it is not easy, because she is a judge of flies.

And you,' he added politely, after a short silence, 'what do you do in peace time?'

'I write a little,' said Aurelle, 'and I am trying for a degree.'

'No, no; I mean what is your sport—fishing, hunting, golf, polo?'

'To tell the truth,' acknowledged Aurelle, 'I am not much good at sport. I am not very strong and——'

'I'm sorry to hear that,' said the major, but he turned to his other neighbour and bothered no more about the Frenchman.

Aurelle was thrown back on the Veterinary Captain Clarke sitting on his left, who had up to then been eating and drinking without saying a word.

'It rains a lot in your country·,' said Captain Clarke.

'So it does in England,' said Aurelle.

'I intend,' said Clarke, 'when this damned war is over to go back to Santa Lucia.'

Aurelle asked if the captain's family lived in the Antilles.

He was horrified.

'Oh, no! I belong to a Staffordshire family. I went out there quite by chance; I was travelling for pleasure and my boat touched at Santa Lucia; I found the heat very agreeable and I stayed there. I bought some land very cheap and I grow cocoa.'

'And it does not bore you?'

'No, the nearest white man is six miles off, and the coast of the island is excellent for sailing. What more could I do at home? When I go to England for three months' holiday, I spend a week at my old home, then I go off in a yacht alone. I have been all round your Brittany coast; it is delightful because the currents are so difficult and your charts are so good; but it is not warm enough. At Santa Lucia I can smoke cigarettes in my pyjamas on my veranda.'

He slowly swallowed his port and concluded:

'No, I don't like Europe—too much work. But, out there, there is enough food for everybody.'

The colonel at the other end of the table was holding forth about India, the white ponies of his regiment, the native servants with their complicated names and varied duties, and the lax life in the Hills. Parker described hunting on an elephant.

'You stand up on your animal firmly tied on by one leg, and when the elephant gallops you fly into space; it's really most exciting.'

'I'll take your word for it,' said Aurelle.

'Yes, but if you try it,' said the colonel solicitously to Aurelle, 'don't forget to slide off by the tail as quickly as you can if the elephant comes to marshy ground. His instinct, when the ground gives way beneath him, is to seize you in his trunk and put you down in front of him to have something solid to kneel on.'

'I'll remember, sir,' said Aurelle.

'In the Malay States,' said the major of Engineers, 'the wild elephants wander about the main roads. I often met them when I was on my motor-bike; if your face or clothes annoy them they pick you off and smash your head by treading on it. But except for that they are quite inoffensive.'

A long discussion on the most vulnerable part of an elephant followed. The padre showed his knowledge by explaining how the anatomy of the Indian elephant differed from that of the African species.

'Padre,' said Aurelle, 'I always knew you were a

sportsman; but have you ever really done any big game shooting?'

'What! my dear fellow? Big game? I've killed pretty nearly everything a hunter *can* kill, from the elephant and rhinoceros to the lion and tiger. I've never told you the story of my first lion?'

'Never, padre,' said the doctor, 'but you are going to now.'

'Padre,' said the colonel, 'I should like to hear your stories, but I make one condition: some one must start the gramophone for me. I want my dear "Mrs Finzi-Magrini" tonight.'

'Oh, no, sir, for pity's sake! I'll let you have a rag-time if you absolutely must grind that damned machine.'

'Not at all, doctor, you aren't going to get off so easily. I insist on "Finzi-Magrini". Come, Aurelle, like a good chap, and remember, speed 65, and don't scratch my record. Padre, you may now begin the story of your first lion.'

'I was at Johannesburg and very much wanted to join a sporting club, as a number of the members were friends of mine. But the rules did not admit any candidate who had not at least killed a lion. So I set out with a nigger loaded with several rifles, and that evening lay in wait with him near a water-hole where a lion was accustomed to come and drink.

'Half an hour before midnight I heard the crashing of branches and over the top of a bush appeared the head of a lion. He had winded us and looked our way. I aimed and fired. The head disappeared behind the bush, but appeared again after a minute. A second shot, the same result. The brute got frightened, hid his head and then put it up again. I remained quite cool, I had sixteen shots to fire in my various rifles. Third shot, same old game; fourth shot, ditto.

'I got unnerved and shot badly, so that after the fifteenth shot the beast put up his head again. "Miss that one, him eat us," said the nigger. I took a long breath, aimed carefully and fired. The animal fell. One second—two—ten—he did not reappear. I waited a little longer, then I rushed out followed by my nigger, and guess, messiou, what I found behind.'

'The lion, padre.'

'*Sixteen* lions, my boy, and every one had a bullet in its eye! That's how I made my debut.'

'By Jove, padre! Who says the Scotch have no imagination?'

'Now listen to a true story. It was in India that I first killed a woman. Yes, yes, a woman! I had set out tiger-shooting when in passing through a village, buried in the jungle, an old native stopped me. "Sahib, sahib, a bear!" And he pointed out a moving black shape up a tree. I took aim quickly and fired. The mass fell heavily with a crashing of branches, and I discovered an old woman, whom I had demolished while she was picking fruit. Another old nigger, the husband, overwhelmed me with abuse. They went and fetched the native police-man. I had to buy off the family; it cost a terrible lot, at least two pounds.

'The story soon got about for twenty miles round, and for several weeks I could not go through a village without two or three old men rushing at me and crying, "Sahib, sahib, a bear up the tree!" I need hardly tell you that they had just made their wives climb up.'

Then Parker described a crocodile hunt, and Captain Clarke gave some details about sharks in Bermuda, which are not dangerous as long as people take the precaution of jumping into the water in company. The colonel, meanwhile, played 'The March of the Lost Brigade' in slow time. The New Zealand major put some eucalyptus leaves in the fire so that the smell might remind him of the Bush. Aurelle, rather dazed, fuddled with the Indian sun and the scent of wild animals, at last realized that this world is a great park laid out by a gardener god for the gentlemen of the United Kingdoms.

CHAPTER VII

POETRY IS RHYMED FOOLISHNESS

Since you are kept indoors beside the ember,
Since you despise the novels on your lists,
Since, happily, no happy man exists,
And since this August wickedly persists
      To play December;

I scribble you these lines sans form or feet,
Sans rhyme—and reason, which one more deplores,
Which I shall call, when stand my works complete,
'Talk with a lady who was kept indoors
      By rain and sleet.'

I know not if your sentiment's the same,
But when I idly sit, in idle dreams,
And the rain falls upon my heart, it seems . . .

'Aurelle,' said the doctor, 'this time you *are* writing verses; deny it if you can. You are taken red-handed.'

'M-ph!' grunted the colonel scornfully, but with indulgence.

'I own to it, doctor, but what then? Is it contrary to King's Regulations?'

'No,' said the doctor, 'but I'm surprised. I have always been convinced that the French cannot be a nation of poets. Poetry is rhymed foolishness. Now you are not a fool, and you have no sense of rhythm.'

'You do not know our poets,' said Aurelle, annoyed. 'Have you read Musset, Hugo, Baudelaire?'

'I know Hugo,' said the colonel. 'When I commanded the troops in Guernsey I was shown his house. I also tried to read his book, "The Toilers of the Sea", but it was too boring.'

The arrival of Major Parker, pushing in front of him two boyish-looking captains, put an end to this conference.

'Here are young Gibbons and Warburton. You must give them a cup of tea before sending them back to their companies. I found them sitting on the side of the Zillebeke Road, no doubt waiting for a taxi. These London people will expect anything.'

Gibbons was returning from leave, and Warburton, a dark Welshman very like a Frenchman who had been wounded two months before in Artois, was rejoining the Lennox after sick leave.

'Aurelle, give me a cup of tea like a good fellow,' said Major Parker. 'Oh, the milk first, I beseech you! And ask for a whisky and soda to wake up Captain Gibbons, will you? He looks as if he had just come out of his wigwam and had not dug up his war hatchet yet.'

'It's such a horrible change,' said Gibbons. 'Yesterday morning I was still in my garden in a real English valley, with hedges and trees. Everything was clean and fresh and cared-for and happy. My pretty sisters-in-law were playing tennis. We were all dressed in white, and here I am suddenly transported into this dreadful mangled wood among you band of assassins. When *do* you think this damned war will be over? I am such a peaceable man! I prefer church bells to guns and the piano to a Hotchkiss. My one ambition is to live in the country with my plump little wife and a lot of plump little children.' And, raising his glass, he concluded, 'I drink to the end of these follies, and to hell with the Boches who brought us here!'

But keen Warburton cut in immediately.

'I like the War. It is only War that gives us a normal existence. What do you do in peace-time? You stay at home; you don't know what to do with your time; you argue with your parents, and your wife—if you have one. Everyone thinks you are an insufferable egotist— and so you are. The War comes; you only go home every five or six months. You are a hero, and, what women appreciate much more, you are a change. You know stories that have never been published. You've seen strange men and terrible things. Your father, instead of telling his friends that you are embittering the end of his life, introduces you to them as an oracle. These old men consult you on foreign politics. If you are married, your wife is prettier than ever; if you are not, all the girls lay siege to you.

'You like the country? Well, you live in a wood here. You love your wife? But who was it said that it is easier to die for the woman one loves than to live with her? For myself I prefer a Hotchkiss to the piano, and the chatter of my men to that of the old ladies who come to tea at my home. No, Gibbons, War is a wonderful epoch,' and, holding up his glass, he said, 'I drink to the gentle Hun who procures these pleasures for us.'

Then he described his time at the Duchess' hospital.

'I thought I was with the Queen of the Fairies. We got everything we wanted without asking for it. When our fiancées were coming to see us, we were propped up with cushions to match the colour of our eyes. A fortnight before I could get up, they brought twelve brightly coloured dressing-gowns for me to choose which one I would wear the first time I was allowed out of bed. I chose a red and green one, which was hung up near me, and I was in such a hurry to put it on that I got well three days quicker. There was a Scotch captain with such a beautiful wife that all the patients' temperatures went up when she came to see him. They ended by making a special door for her near her husband's bed, so that she need not walk down the whole ward. Oh, I hope I shall be wounded soon! Doctor, promise to send me to the Duchess' hospital!'

But Gibbons, with eyes still full of tender memories of home, would not be consoled. The padre, who was wise and kind, made him describe the last revue at the Palace, and complacently discussed the legs and shoulders of a 'sweet little thing.' The colonel got out his best records and played 'Mrs Finzi-Magrini' and 'Destiny Waltz' to his guests. Gibbons sat with his head in his hands during the waltz. The colonel was going to chaff him mildly about his melancholy thoughts, but the little captain got up at the end of the tune and said:

'I had better be off before dark.'

'Silly ass,' said Parker, after a pause.

The colonel and the padre agreed. Aurelle alone protested.

'Aurelle, my friend,' said Dr O'Grady, 'if you want to be thought anything of amongst Englishmen, you must make yourself see their point of view. They don't care for melancholy people, and have a contempt for sentiment. This applies to love as well as to patriotism and religion. If you want the colonel to despise you, stick a flag in your tunic. If you want the padre to treat

[54]

you with contempt, give him a letter to censor full of pious rubbish; if you want to make Parker sick, weep over a photograph. They spend their youth hardening their skins and their hearts. They fear neither physical blows nor the blows of fate. They look upon exaggeration as the worst of vices, and coldness as a sign of aristocracy. When they are very miserable, they smile. When they are very happy, they say nothing at all. And *au fond* John Bull is terribly sentimental, which explains everything.'

'All that is perfectly true, Aurelle,' said Parker, 'but you must not say it. The doctor is a confounded Irishman who cannot hold his tongue.'

Upon which, the doctor and Major Parker began a discussion on the Irish question in their usual amusingly sarcastic manner. The colonel looked in his box of records for 'When Irish eyes are smiling,' then wisely and courteously interrupted them.

'And so, Aurelle,' concluded Major Parker, 'you see us poor Englishmen searching hard for the solution of a problem when there isn't one. You may think that the Irish want certain definite reforms, and that they will be happy and contented the day they get them; but not at all. What amuses them is discussion itself, plotting in theory. They play with the idea of Home Rule; if we gave it them, the game would be finished and they would invent another, probably a more dangerous one.'

'Go to Ireland after the War, messiou,' said the colonel, 'it's an extraordinary country. Every one is mad. You can commit the worst crimes—it doesn't matter. Nothing matters.'

'The worst crimes?' said Aurelle. 'Oh, I say, sir!'

'Oh, yes, anything you like—the most unheard-of

things. You can go out hunting in brown breeches, fish in your neighbour's salmon river—nothing will happen; no one will take the smallest notice of you.'

'I do believe,' said Aurelle, 'that I am beginning to understand the Irish question.'

'I will finish your education,' said the doctor. 'A year before the War a Liberal M.P. who was visiting Ireland said to an old peasant, "Well, my friend, we are soon going to give you Home Rule!" "God save us, your honour," said the man, "do not do that." "What?" said the astonished Member. "You don't want Home Rule now?" "Your honour," said the man, "I'll tell you. You are a good Christian, your honour? It's to heaven you want to go? So do I, but we do not want to go there tonight." '

CHAPTER VIII

0275 PRIVATE SCOTT

CHORUS: 'What, Jupiter not so strong as these goddesses?'
PROMETHEUS: 'Yes, even he cannot escape destiny.'

When young Lieutenant Warburton, temporarily commanding B Company of the Lennox Highlanders, took over his trench, the captain he came to relieve said to him:

'This part is not too unhealthy; they are only thirty yards off, but they are tame Boches. All they ask is to be left alone.'

'We will wake things up a bit,' said Warburton to his men, when the peaceable warrior had departed.

When wild beasts are too well fed, they become domesticated; but a few well-directed rockets will make them savage again. In virtue of this principle, Warburton, having provided himself with a star shell, instead of sending it straight up fired it horizontally towards the German trenches.

A distracted Saxon sentry cried, 'Liquid-fire attack!' The Boche machine-guns began to bark. Warburton, delighted, replied with grenades. The enemy called the artillery to its assistance. A telephone call, a hail of shrapnel, and immediate reprisals by the British big guns.

The next day the German *communiqué* said: 'An attack by the British under cover of liquid-fire at H—— was completely checked by the combined fire of our infantry and artillery.'

0275 Private Scott, H. J., who served his King and country under the strenuous Warburton, disapproved heartily of his officer's heroic methods. Not that he was a coward, but the War had taken him by surprise when he had just married a charming girl, and, as Captain Gadsby of the Pink Hussars says, 'a married man is only half a man.' Scott counted the days he spent in the trenches, and this one was the first of ten, and his chief was reckless.

The god who guards lovers intervened the next day by the simple means of a scrap of paper asking for a man from the regiment, mechanic by trade, to look after a machine at P—— for disinfecting clothes. P—— was a pretty little town at least eight miles from the front line, rather deserted by the inhabitants on account of *marmites*, but all the same a safe and comfortable retreat for a troglodyte of the trenches.

0275 Private Scott, mechanic by trade, put his name down. His lieutenant abused him; his colonel recommended him; and his general nominated him. An old London omnibus painted a military grey took him away to his new life, far from Warburton and his perils.

The machine which Scott had to look after was in the yard of a college, an old building covered with ivy; and Abbé Hoboken, the principal, received him, when he arrived, as if he were a general.

'Are you a Catholic, my son?' he asked him in the English of the college.

Luckily for Scott, he did not understand, and answered vaguely:

'Yes, sir.'

This involuntary renunciation of the Scotch Presbyterian Church procured him a room belonging to a mobilized Belgian professor and a bed with sheets.

Now, at that very moment, Hauptmann Reineker, who commanded a German battery of heavy artillery at Paschendaele, was in a very bad temper.

The evening post had brought him an ambiguous letter from his wife in which she mentioned too often, and with an affection of indifference, a wounded officer of the Guards, whom she had been nursing for several days.

During the night, he surveyed his gun-emplacements on the outskirts of a wood, then he said suddenly:

'Wolfgang, have you any shells available?'

'Yes, sir.'

'How many?'

'Three.'

'Good! Wake up Theresa's crew.'

He then verified his calculations by his map.

The men, half awake, loaded the enormous gun. Reineker gave the order, and, shaking up everyone and everything, the shell started forth, hurtling through the night.

0275 Private Scott, then, who adored his wife and had accepted a post without honour for her sake, was sleeping peacefully in the bedroom of a mobilized Belgian professor: and Captain Reineker, whose wife no longer loved him, and whom he mistrusted, was striding furiously up and down amongst the frozen woods; and these two circumstances, widely apart from one another, were developed independently in an indifferent world.

Now the calculations of Reineker, like most calculations, went wrong. He was 400 yards out. His landmark was the church. From the church to the college was 400 yards. A light wind increased the deviation by 20 yards, and from that moment the Reineker and the Scott situation began to have points in common. At this particular point the chest of 0275 Private Scott received the full force of the ·305 shell, and he was blown into a thousand bits, which, amongst other things, put an end to the Scott situation.

CHAPTER IX

ON PADRES AND PADRES

'The ideal of the English Church has been to provide a resident gentleman for every parish in the Kingdom, and there have been worse ideals.'
SHANE LESLIE

Aurelle, arriving for tea at the Mess, found only the padre repairing a magic lantern.

'Hullo, messiou,' he said, 'very glad to see you. I am getting my lantern ready for a sporting sermon to the men of B Company when they come out of the trenches.'

'What, padre, you preach sermons now with a magic lantern?'

'My boy, I am trying to make the men come; there are too many who keep away. I know very well that the regiment has a good many Presbyterians, but if you could see the Irish regiments—not a man misses going to Mass. Ah, messiou, the Catholic padres have more influence than we have. I ask myself, why? I go every day to the trenches, and even if the men think me an old fool they might at least recognize that I am a sportsman.'

'The regiment is very fond of you, padre. But, if you don't mind me saying so, I think that Catholic priests have a special influence. Confession has something to do with it, but their vow of celibacy more, because, in a sort of way, it makes them different from other people. Even the doctor tones down his best stories when Father Murphy dines with us.'

'But, my boy, I love O'Grady's stories; I am an old soldier and a man of the world. When I was shooting in Africa a negro queen made me a present of three young negresses.'

'Padre!'

'Oh, I let them go the same day, which annoyed them somewhat. But I don't see why, after that, I need play Mrs Grundy in the Mess.'

One of the orderlies brought some boiling water, and the padre asked Aurelle to make the tea.

'When I was married—*not* that way, messiou; it's curious that no Frenchman can make tea. Always warm the teapot first, my boy; you cannot make good tea with a cold teapot.'

'You were talking about your wedding, padre.'

'Yes, I wanted to tell you how indignant all these Pharisees were, who want me to behave like a prude with young people, when I merely wanted to be reasonable. When I was going to be married, I naturally had to ask one of my colleagues to perform the ceremony. After having settled the important points, I said to him, "In the Marriage Service of the Church of England there is one passage which I consider absolutely indecent. Yes, yes, I know quite well that it is what St Paul said. Well, probably in his time he had a perfect right to say such things, and they were adapted to the manners and customs of the Corinthians, but they are not meant for the ears of a young girl from Aberdeen in 1906. My fiancée is innocent, and I will not have her shocked." The young man, a worldly-minded little curate, went and complained to the bishop, who sent for me and said haughtily, "So it is *you* who are taking upon yourself to forbid the reading of the Epistle to the Corinthians? I would have you know that I am not the man to put up with nonsense of this sort." "All right," I replied, "I would have you know that I am not the man to put up with an insult to my wife. If this fellow insists on reading the passage I shall say nothing in the church, out of respect for the sacred edifice, but I promise you that after the ceremony I shall box his ears."

'Well, messiou, the bishop looked at me carefully to see if I was in earnest. Then he remembered my campaign in the Transvaal, the negro Queen, and the dangers of a scandal, and he answered me with unction, "I do not see after all that the passage that shocks you is absolutely essential to the marriage ceremony." '

Dr O'Grady here came in and asked for a cup of tea.

'Who made this tea?' he demanded. 'You, Aurelle? How much tea did you put in?'

'One spoonful for each cup.'

'Now listen to an axiom—one spoonful for each cup and then one for the pot. It is curious that no Frenchman knows how to make tea.'

Aurelle changed the subject.

'The padre was telling me about his wedding.'

'A padre ought not to be married,' said the doctor. 'You know what St Paul said, "A married man seeks to please his wife and not God." '

'You have put your foot in it now,' said Aurelle. 'Don't talk to him about St Paul; he has just been strafing him badly.'

'Excuse me,' said the padre, 'I only strafed a bishop.'

'Padre,' said the doctor, 'judge not——'

'Oh, I know,' said the padre, 'the Master said that, but He did not know any bishops.' Then he turned to his old subject. 'Tell me, O'Grady, you are Irish; why have the Catholic chaplains more influence than we?'

'Padre,' said the doctor, 'listen to a parable. It is your turn. A man had committed a murder. He was not suspected, but remorse made him restless and miserable. One day, as he was passing an Anglican church, it seemed to him that the secret would be easier to bear if he could share it with someone else, so he entered and asked the vicar to hear his confession.

'The vicar was a very well brought up young man, and had been at Eton and Oxford. Enchanted with this rare piece of luck, he said eagerly, "Most certainly, open your heart to me; you can talk to me as if I were your father!" The other began: "I have killed a man." The vicar sprang to his feet. "And you come here to tell *me* that? Horrible murderer! I am not sure that it is not my duty as a citizen to take you to the nearest police station. In any case it is my duty as a gentleman not to keep you a moment longer under my roof."

'And the man went away. A few miles farther on he saw a Roman Catholic church. A last hope made him enter, and he knelt down behind some old women who were waiting by the confessional. When his turn came he could just distinguish the priest praying in the shadows, his head in his hands. "Father," he said, "I am not a Catholic, but I should like to confess to you." "I am listening, my son." "Father, I have committed murder."

'He awaited the effect of this terrible revelation. In the austere silence of the church the voice of the priest said simply, "How many times, my son?"'

'Doctor,' said the padre, 'you know that I am Scotch. I can only take in a story a week after I hear it.'

'That one will take you longer, padre,' said the doctor.

CHAPTER X

AWARD FOR VALOUR

S. W. Tarkington, an officer of fifty-three, honorary lieutenant and quartermaster, was possessed of a vain but keen desire to win one more ribbon before retiring. The laws of nature and eighteen years of good conduct had given him the South African medal and the long service ribbon. But with a little luck even an honorary lieutenant may pick up a Military Cross if the bullets fall in the right place. That is why Tarkington was always to be found in dangerous corners where he had no business, and that is why, on the day Loos was taken, he wandered with his rheumatic old joints over the soaking battlefield and carried in eighteen wounded men on his back. But he met no general and no one knew anything about it, except the wounded, who have no influence.

From there the regiment was sent to the north and went into the line in the Ypres salient. There existed, no doubt, excellent sentimental and military reasons for defending this piece of ground, but as a winter residence it left much to be desired. Tarkington did not fear the danger—shells were part of the day's work—but his rheumatism feared the water, and the rain falling incessantly on the greasy clay made a damp and icy paste which no doctor would recommend for the oiling of old joints. Tarkington, whose painfully swollen feet now made the shortest march a Chinese torture, finally realized that he must apply to be sent to hospital.

'It's just my luck,' he said to his confidant, the sergeant-major. 'I have the pain without the wound.'

So he went off limping and swearing to find the colonel in his dug-out, and told him of the state of his legs.

The colonel was in a bad temper that morning. A communication from the headquarters of the division had pointed out to him that the proportion of trench feet in his regiment had reached 3·6 per cent, whereas the average of the corps was only 2·7. And would he take the necessary precautions to reduce his percentage in the future?

The necessary precautions had been taken; he had sent for the doctor and given him the communication.

'And see here, O'Grady. You may have bronchitis, sore throats and gastric enteritis, but I do not want any more trench feet for three days.'

You may imagine how Tarkington was received when he came to exhibit his paralysed feet.

'Now that's the limit. *I* send down an officer for trench feet? Read, Tarkington, read, and do you imagine I am going to transform 3·5 into 3·6 to please *you*? Look up, my friend, General Routine Orders No. 324—"Trench Feet result from a contraction of the superficial arteries with the consequence that the skin no longer being nourished dies and mortifies." Therefore, all you have to do is to watch your arteries. Tarkington, I am extremely sorry, old man, but that is all I can do for you.'

'Just my luck,' said the old man to his friend the sergeant-major. 'I have thirty-seven years' service; I have never been ill; and when, for the first time in my life,

I ask for sick leave, it happens on the very same day that headquarters have strafed the colonel over that very subject.'

His feet became red, then blue, and had begun to turn black when the colonel went away on leave. The command in his absence was taken over by Major Parker who, being the second son of a peer, paid small attention to remarks from the brigade. He saw the distress of the unfortunate Tarkington, and sent him to the field hospital, where they decided to send him to England. It seemed that Tarkington was not the kind to be acclimatized in the Flemish marshes.

He was taken to B—— and put on board the hospital ship *Saxonia*, with the wounded, doctors and nurses. The port officials had ascertained to their annoyance the day before that a number of floating mines were in the Channel.

The authorities argued over the origin of these mines, which the N.T.O. said were those of the Allies, while the M.L.O. thought they were the enemy's. But there was no argument about one detail; every boat that had come into contact with one had been cut in two and sunk immediately.

The captain of the *Saxonia* was convinced that the Channel was free from mines. He risked it—and was blown up.

So Tarkington jumped into the sea. As a good soldier, his instinct was to devote his last minutes to keeping calm, and he swam about quietly with the gas mask that he had been advised never to lose hanging round his neck.

A salvage boat picked him up, unconscious, and he was taken to a hospital on the English coast. He recovered consciousness, but felt very ill from his immersion in the water.

'Just like my cursed luck!' he groaned. 'They stop me starting for a month, and when at last I do get off, it is in the only ship that has gone down for a year.'

'They are all alike,' said the colonel, on his return from leave. 'Here's a blighter who grumbles at having his feet in water, and then takes advantage of my absence to go and have a salt-water bath!'

Now, a few months before, King George, after his accident in France, had crossed the Channel on board the *Saxonia*. The fate of the ship naturally interested His Majesty, who came to see the survivors, and, as Tarkington was the only officer, he had the inestimable privilege of quite a long conversation with the King. The result of this was that a few days afterwards a regiment 'somewhere in France' received a memorandum from general headquarters asking for a statement of the services of Tarkington, S. W.

The memorandum being accompanied by certain verbal comments on the subject of 'a very distinguished personage' by an officer in a red-banded gold-peaked cap, the colonel wrote nice things—which he had never said to him—of Tarkington, S. W., and the sergeant-major gave details of the brilliant conduct of the quartermaster at Loos.

The *London Gazette* a fortnight later recapitulated these exploits in a supplement to the list of awards and honours, and Tarkington, honorary captain, M.C., meditating on his fate, found the world not such a bad place after all.

CHAPTER XI

THE BRIGADE AND THE VILLAGE

The first encounter that the brigade had with the village was not happy.

The village looked distrustfully on the brigade, with its bare knees and its language like the rolling of a drum. The brigade found the village short of *estaminets* and pretty girls. The people of Hondezeele bewailed the departure of a division of London Territorials, with their soft voices and full pockets, and wherever Aurelle went they did nothing but sing the praises of these sons of their adoption.

'Your Scotsmen, we know them. We cannot understand what they say—and my little girls can speak English.'

'Scotch—Promenade—no bon!' said the little girls.

'I had the general's chauffeur here,' went on the old woman, 'a nice boy, sir. Billy, they called him. He washed up for me, and pleasant spoken, too, and good manners. An officers' Mess? Certainly not. I can make more selling fried potatoes and beer to the boys, and even eggs, although they cost me threepence each.'

'Fried potatoes, two painnies a plate, aigs and bacon, one franc,' chorused the little girls.

Aurelle went on to the next house, where other old women mourned other Billys, Harrys, Gingers, and Darkies.

One stout lady explained that noise gave her palpitations; another, quite seventy-five, that it was not proper for a girl living alone.

At last he found a corpulent lady whom he overwhelmed with such eloquent protestations that she could not get in a word. The next morning, he sent her the orderlies with the plate and crockery, and at lunchtime brought along Parker and O'Grady. The servants were waiting for them at the door.

'Madame is a regular witch, sir. She's a proper fury, that's what she is, sir.'

'Madame' welcomed them with confused complaints.

'Ah! bien merci! Ah! bien merci! How I have regretted having agreed to have you. I have not had a wink of sleep with my husband abusing me. He nearly beat me, monsieur. Oh, don't touch that! I forbid you to enter my clean kitchen. Wipe your feet, and take those boxes off there!'

'Put the boxes in the dining-room,' ordered Aurelle to conciliate her.

'Thank you! Put your dirty boxes in my dining-room, with my beautiful table and my fine dresser! I should think so, indeed!'

'But, in heaven's name, madame,' said Aurelle quietly, 'where shall I put them?'

He half opened a door at the end of the dining-room.

'Will you kindly leave that door alone! My lovely *salon*, where I do not even go myself for fear of making it dirty! And, besides, I have had enough of your Mess, I'm about tired of it.'

A little later, Aurelle went into Madame Lemaire's, the draper's, to buy some chocolate. She had relegated all her pre-war trade to a corner of the shop, and now sold, like the rest of the village, Quaker Oats, Woodbine cigarettes, and post-cards with the words: 'From your Soldier Boy.'

While she was serving him, Aurelle espied behind the shop a charming, bright little apartment, decorated with plates on the wall, and a clean cloth, with green and white squares, on the table. He strolled carelessly towards the door. Madame Lemaire looked suspiciously at him and folded her arms across her enormous bust.

'Would you believe, madame, that there are in this village people so unpatriotic as to refuse to take in officers, who have no where to eat their meals?'

'Is it possible?' said Madame Lemaire, blushing.

He told her who they were.

'Ah, the carpenter's wife!' said Madame Lemaire, turning up her nose in disgust. 'I am not surprised. They come from Moevekerke, and the people of Moevekerke are all bad.'

'But it seems to me,' insinuated Aurelle gently, 'that you have a room here that would just do.'

.   .   .

A week later the village and the brigade were tasting the pure joys of the honeymoon. In each house a Jack, a Ginger or a Darkey helped to wash up, called the old lady Granny, and joked with the girls. The London Territorials were quite forgotten. At night, in the barns, beribboned bagpipes accompanied the monotonous dances.

Aurelle had lodged the padre at Madame Potiphar's, a lively young widow to whom the divisions, billeted in turn in the village, had handed on this nickname, like a local password.

The virtue of the padre, which had protected him against the solid charms of three young negresses, feared nothing from the manoeuvres of a village Potiphar.

Parker and O'Grady shared a large room in the inn. They called the publican and his wife Papa and Mamma. Lucie and Berthe, the daughters of the house, taught them French. Lucie was six feet high; she was pretty, slender, and fair. Berthe was more substantial and remarkably good-natured. These two fine Flemish girls, honest without prudishness, greedy of gain, lacking in culture but not in shrewdness, were the admiration of Major Parker.

Although their father was in a fair way to making a fortune by selling the Tommies English beer made in France, they never thought of asking him for money for their clothes or for making a servant work in their stead.

'One ought to be able to fight when one leaves such women at home,' said the major admiringly.

The father was the same sort. He described to Aurelle the death of his son, a splendid boy, three times mentioned in despatches. He talked of him with a pride and resignation truly admirable.

Aurelle advised the publican, if he had a few hundred francs to spare to put them in the War Loan.

'I have already put in fifty thousand francs,' said the old man. 'I shall wait a little now.'

The whole village was rich.

Colonel Bramble gave two sous one day to Madame Lemaire's son, an urchin of five or six.

'To buy some sweets with,' Aurelle told him.

'Oh no, I don't care for them.'

'What will you do with your sous, then?'

'Put them in my money-box till I have got enough to

get a deposit book in the Savings Bank; then, when I am grown up, I shall buy some land.'

That evening Aurelle repeated this to Lucie and Berthe, thinking it would amuse them. He soon found out that no one was amused: jokes about money were sacrilege. The publican related a little moral story to make this clear.

'When I was small,' he said, 'I often used to go on messages into the town for Monsieur le curé, and each time he gave me two sous, which I took to my father. But after a time, Monsieur le curé made old Sophie, his servant, send me on his commissions and she never gave me my two sous. My father, who asked me for them, was very indignant. He consulted my grandfather, and the whole family were called in one evening to discuss the matter.

'My father said, "The child cannot go and complain to Monsieur le curé, because if it is he who has stopped the two sous he might be offended." "And if it is old Sophie who has diddled the child out of it she would box his ears," said my mother. My grandfather, who was no fool, hit upon the best way. He said to me, "You will go and make your confession to Monsieur le curé. You will tell him that you have sinned by getting angry with old Sophie because she sent you to the town without giving you anything."

'It was a great success. "What," said the curé. "The old wretch! She charged me for them every time. Release me from the secret of the confessional and I will give her a good talking-to!" I remembered that her hand was heavy and I did not release him; but in future he always sent me himself.'

The schoolmistress from Lille, who possessed the only

piano in the village, explained to Aurelle that she had had to cut out of her lesson the whole chapter on economy and thrift, substituting a lesson on generosity. A little girl of eight then said to her, 'I can never do that, mademoiselle. My mother is mean, and I am sure I shall be meaner than she.'

Meanwhile the Highlanders were turning the King's shillings into glasses of beer, and were showering on these economical little girls embroidered aprons, sugar-plums and post-cards, with 'From Your Soldier Boy' on them, price ninepence.

The plump and active mothers of these nice little Flemish girls sold the aprons and postcards.

'Ah, messiou,' said Colonel Bramble, 'before the War we used to talk about frivolous France; now it is stern and prudent France.'

'Yes,' added the doctor, 'the French are hard and severe on themselves. I begin to understand the Boche who said, "Man does not aspire to happiness, only Englishmen." There is, among your peasants of the north, an admirable voluntary asceticism.'

'Did you ever see, messiou,' said the padre, 'in our country, before the War, the Frenchman of the music-hall? The little fellow with the black beard, who gesticulates and harangues? I believed it, messiou, and never pictured these devout and industrious villagers.'

'I like to see them on Sunday mornings,' said the major, 'when the bell for Mass starts ringing, and they all come out of their houses together, old men, women and children, as if they were going to a theatre. Ah, messiou, why didn't you tell us all about this before the War?'

'The reason is,' said Aurelle, 'that we didn't know it ourselves.'

CHAPTER XII

THE CAPTAIN AND THE
MASKED LADY

Orion's belt rose higher in the wintry sky; the roads were frozen hard. The mail vans overflowed more and more every day with enormous quantities of puddings and Christmas cards, and the festive season recalled the joys of life to the division and the village.

The preparations for the Christmas dinner occupied Aurelle and the padre for some time. The latter found a turkey worthy of the royal table at a farm; Aurelle hunted from house to house for chestnuts; Parker attended himself to the cooking, and mixed a salad of which he was very proud, but the colonel examined it long and doubtfully. As for the doctor, he was sent off with Aurelle to Bailleul to buy some champagne, and insisted on sampling several different brands, which inspired him to give vent to some strange doctrines on things in general on the way home.

He obtained permission to invite his friends Berthe and Lucie to come in at the end of dinner to drink a bumper of champagne in the Mess, and when they entered in their Sunday dresses, the colonel played 'Destiny Waltz', speed 61. The orderlies had hung a great bunch of mistletoe over the door, and the girls asked ingenuously if it was not the custom in England to kiss under the mistletoe.

'Oh, certainly,' said the doctor, and with his hands behind his back, he pecked Berthe on the cheek which she turned towards him. Parker, equally nervous, did the same to pretty Lucie, and Aurelle gave them both a good hug in the French way.

'That's fine, mademoiselle?' said the little doctor.

'Yes,' said Lucie with a sigh. 'We wish it was always Christmas.'

'Oh, but why?' said the doctor.

'Think how dull it will be for us after the War,' replied Berthe, 'when you are all gone! Before, one did not think of it—one saw no one—one worked, one knew no better, but now, without the boys, the village will be empty indeed. My sister and I will not stay here. We will go to Paris or London.'

'Oh, but that's a pity,' said the doctor.

'No, no,' said Aurelle, 'you will just get married. You will marry rich farmers, you will be very busy with your beasts and your chickens and you will forget all about us.'

'It's easy to say "get married",' observed Berthe, 'but it takes two for that. And if there are not enough young men for all the girls we shall probably get left in the lurch.'

'Every man will have several wives,' said Aurelle. 'You will be much happier; with one husband between you two; you will only have half the housework to do.'

'I do not think I should like it,' said Lucie, who was very refined.

But the padre, to whom the doctor had just treacherously translated Aurelle's cynical proposals, indignantly protested.

'*You* ought not to criticize polygamy, padre,' said the

[76]

doctor. 'Re-read your Bible. What have you to say about old Laban, who, having sold his two daughters to the same man, payable monthly for fourteen years, gave the purchaser in addition two waiting-maids as a bonus.'

'But,' said the padre, 'I am not responsible for the actions of a doubtful patriarch. I have no sympathy with Laban.'

'No more have I,' said Aurelle. 'This Dufayel of marriage has always profoundly disgusted me, but more on account of his matrimonial methods than for having gone in for the polygamy natural to his tribe. Moreover, is the number of women to be apportioned to one man a question of morals ? It appears to me to be a question of arithmetic. If there are nearly as many women as men, monogamy is the rule; if for some reason the number of women is increased, polygamy is perhaps better for the general welfare.'

The two girls, who understood this conversation much less than the 'promenade' and the 'na poo' of the Tommies, went up to the colonel, who talked to them paternally in his gruff way and got the 'Caruso' record for them out of its pink cover.

'You have some weird ideas about animal psychology, Aurelle,' said the doctor. 'If you have observed nature, you would have proved, on the contrary, that the question of the numbers of mates is certainly not a question of arithmetic. With gnats, ten females are born to one male. Now gnats are not polygamous. Nine of those females die spinsters. It is only the old maids who bite us, from which one sees that celibacy engenders ferocity among insects as well as among women.'

'I have known some charming old maids,' said Aurelle.

'Indeed!' said the doctor. 'But, however that may be,

the number of married pairs varies simply according to the way the species feed. Rabbits, Turks, sheep, artists, and, generally speaking, all herbivorous creatures are polygamous; while foxes, Englishmen, wolves, bankers, and, generally speaking, all carnivorous animals are monogamists. That is because of the difficulty which carnivorous animals find in rearing their young until they are strong enough to kill for themselves. As for polyandry, it occurs in wretched countries like Tibet, where several men must unite forces to keep one wife and her progeny.'

The howls of Caruso rendered all conversation impossible for a minute, then Aurelle said to Lucie:

'The other girls in the village will perhaps find it difficult to get husbands, it is true, but you and your sister need not worry; you are the prettiest, and you will soon have the richest father. You will have fine marriage portions.'

'Yes, that's true. Perhaps they will marry us for our money,' said Berthe, who was modest.

'I should not care to be married for my money,' said Lucie.

'Oh, strange creature!' said the doctor, 'you would like to be loved for your face alone, that is to say, for the position in space of the albuminoids and fatty molecules placed there by the working of some Mendelian heredity, but you would dislike to be loved for your fortune, to which you have contributed by your labour and your domestic virtues.'

Berthe regarded the doctor nervously and reminded her sister that they had some glasses to wash before going to bed; so they emptied their bumpers and departed.

After a restful silence, Major Parker asked Aurelle to

explain the institution of the marriage *dot*, and, when he had grasped it, indignantly replied:

'What? A man receives this splendid gift, a pretty woman, and he exacts money before accepting her? But what you tell me is monstrous, Aurelle, and dangerous. Instead of marrying beautiful and good women who would have beautiful and good children, you marry ugly, quarrelsome creatures provided with a cheque-book.'

' "He who has found a good wife has found great happiness," ' quoted the padre, ' "but a quarrelsome woman is like a roof that lets in the rain." '

'It is wrong to suppose the children of love-matches better made than others,' interrupted the doctor, becoming rather warlike, obviously owing to champagne. 'Oh, I know the old theory: every man chooses his natural complement, and thus rears children which revert to the average type of the race. Big men like little women, large noses like little snub-noses, and very feminine men fall in love with Amazons.

'As a matter of fact, a nervous, short-sighted, intellectual man marries a pedantic, nervous, short-sighted woman because their tastes are similar. Good riders make acquaintance with girls who hunt, and marry them for their sporting tastes.

'So, far from reverting to the average type, love-matches tend to exaggerate the differences. And then is it desirable for selection to operate? There are very few really brilliant men who have not had at least one mad-man among their ancestors. The modern world has been founded by three epileptics—Alexander, Julius Caesar and Luther, without mentioning Napoleon, who was not altogether well balanced.'

'In a thousand men of genius, how many mad relations?' asked the colonel.

'I can't tell you, sir,' said the doctor.

'You can talk nonsense to your heart's content, doctor,' said Major Parker. 'But as far as I am concerned, if I ever marry, I shall only marry a very pretty woman. What's the name of that charming cinema actress we saw together at Hazebrouck, Aurelle?'

'Napierkowska, sir.'

'Oh yes. Well, if I knew her I would marry her at once. And I am sure that she is if anything better and more intelligent than the average woman.'

'My friend Shaw,' said the doctor, 'says that to desire to be perpetually in the society of a pretty woman, until the end of one's days, is as if, because one likes good wine, one wished always to have one's mouth full of it.'

'Rather a flimsy argument,' observed the major. 'For surely that is better than having it always full of bad wine.'

'Anyhow,' the doctor replied, 'women who exhibit more surely than us the underlying instincts of mankind are far from bearing out your theory; I know very few who make a point of marrying a good-looking man.'

'Well, do you know the story about Frazer?' said the major.

'Which Frazer?' said the colonel. 'G.R. of the 60th?'

'No, no. A.K. of the 5th Gurkhas—the one who played polo for the regiment in 1900, an awfully good-looking fellow, the finest chin in the army.'

'Oh, I know him,' said the colonel, 'the son of old Sir Thomas. His father sold me a damned good pony, when I was a subaltern, and I only paid 200 rupees for it. Well, what is his story?'

'At the beginning of 1915,' said the major, 'Frazer, who was crossing London on his way home on leave, went to the theatre one evening alone. Towards the end of the first act, he felt vaguely that some one was staring at him. He looked up and saw a woman in a box looking at him. But, owing to the darkness of the theatre, he could not distinguish her features.

'In the interval, he tried to see her, but she had withdrawn to the back of her box. During the next two acts she looked at him fixedly. Frazer, decidedly intrigued, was waiting at the exit of the theatre, when a magnificent footman approached him, saying, "A lady wishes to speak to you, sir," and led him to the door of a carriage which had stopped in a side street.

' "You do not know me, Captain Frazer," said a very pretty voice, "but I know you; have you anything to do this evening or will you come to supper with me?" Frazer did what we should all have done.'

'He ran away?' said the padre.

'He got into the carriage,' said Parker. 'He was asked to allow himself to be blindfolded. When the bandage was taken off he found himself in a charming room, alone with the fair unknown, who was *décolletée* and wearing a mask, and who had the most beautiful shoulders in the world.'

'Is this by Dumas *père* or R. L. Stevenson?' asked Aurelle.

'It is a story of what actually happened in January, 1915, and was told me by a man who never lies,' said Major Parker. 'The house was in silence. No servant appeared, but Frazer, delighted, was offered by the unknown herself what you French call, I believe, *bon souper, bon gîte et le reste.*

'At break of day, she bandaged his eyes again. He told her how much he had enjoyed himself and asked her when he could see her again. "Never," she replied, "and I take it that I have your word of honour as a gentleman and a soldier that you will never try to find me again. But in one year from now, to the day, go back to the same theatre where we met, and there will, perhaps, be a letter for you." Then she saw him into the carriage again, and asked him to keep his eyes blindfolded for ten minutes: when he took off the bandage, he was in Trafalgar Square.

'Frazer naturally moved heaven and earth to get leave in January, 1916, and on the evening of the anniversary of his adventure appeared at the box office of the theatre and asked for a stall. "Have you by any chance a letter for me?" he said, giving his name. The clerk handed him an envelope, and Frazer, eagerly opening it, read this short line: "It is a fine boy. Thank you." '

'What is still more strange,' said the doctor with sarcasm, 'is that another good-looking lad told me the same story some time before the war, and that that time he was the hero of it.'

'Then this lady must have several children,' said the colonel.

CHAPTER XIII

A POEM

You, pretty shopgirl, whose fresh charm
  Was once engrossing,
And you, who kept, with strong bare arm,
  The level-crossing,

And you, the Teacher, you who went
  In dress less candid,
Or, soft-eyed, o'er your keyboard leant,
  And slender-handed;

Fair Baker's wife, who had our love,
  Yet counted pence
As one who had a soul above
  Their vulgar sense;

All you whose wayside smile could then
  So quickly chase
The black despond of us poor men
  Those hateful days!

Who sprawled across your open door
  And loosed their speech
To tell of hopes and plans in store,
  Beyond their reach. . . .

You did not always understand,
But never mind,
No wiser they, the glitt'ring band
We left behind.

No man but thinks his worth impressed
Where he desires;
And there, as in a mirror drest,
Himself admires.

And Margot, to his talk resigned,
One ear in guile lent,
A very Sévigné he'll find
So she be silent.

CHAPTER XIV

EXTRACTS FROM AURELLE'S DIARY

Madame Lemaire has presented the Mess with a bottle of old brandy, and the doctor is in very good form this evening. He is the true Irish type; a lover of surprising epigrams.

He says, 'We owe to the Middle Ages the two worst inventions of humanity—romantic love and gunpowder.' Again, 'The whole reason of this War is because the Germans have no sense of humour.'

But, above all, you must hear his scientific and precise demonstration of his favourite theory: 'Two telegrams contrary in sense, and from officers equal in rank, cancel one another.'

January 4th.

Rode with the colonel and Parker. How delicate and clear the atmosphere is in this northern part of France! The colonel was highly indignant to hear that I have never been out hunting.

'You *must*, messiou, it is the only sport. You jump banks as high as your horse. At eighteen I had nearly broken my neck twice. It is most exciting.'

'Yes,' said Parker, 'one day I was galloping in a wood and a branch went into my right eye. It is a miracle I wasn't killed. Another time——'

He described how his horse fell on the top of him and broke two of his ribs. Then both of them together, certain of having convinced me:

'You must hunt after the War, messiou.'

January 7th.

This morning, I do not know why, some French troops came through Hondezeele. The village and I were delighted. We like the shrill bagpipes, but no music in the world is like 'Sidi-Brahim' and 'Sambre-et-Meuse.'

I was pleased, too, to be able to show Parker these *Chasseurs à pied*, as all he had seen of our army were old Territorials. He was much impressed.

'They are as fine as the Highlanders,' he told me.

And then he described the Lennox as they were when he joined as second lieutenant in Egypt.

'I was forbidden to speak at Mess for six months. An excellent practice! It taught us to realize how humble we were, and the respect due to our elders.

'If some "swelled head" did not conform to these rules, he soon found his things all packed up in his room, labelled for England. If he still refused to understand, he was called up before a subaltern's court-martial, and heard some home truths about himself.

'It was hard, but what *esprit de corps* and what discipline those rough ways taught us. We shall never see a regiment again like the Lennox of 1914. The officer of today has seen active service, it's true, but as a matter of fact it is quite sufficient in war to have good health and no more imagination than a fish. It is in peace-time that one ought to judge a soldier.'

'You remind me,' said the doctor, 'of the sergeant-major in the Guards who said: "How I wish the war would finish so that we could have real manoeuvres once more!" '

This evening, while the gramophone was raging, I forced myself to translate into French Rudyard Kipling's admirable poem, 'If'.

I showed it in English to Parker whom it describes so well, and we talked about books. I made the mistake of mentioning Dickens.

'I detest Dickens,' said the major. 'I never could understand how anyone could find him interesting. His books are all stories of the lower classes and Bohemians. I do not want to know how they live. In the whole of Dickens' works there is not one gentleman. No, if you wish to know the *chef-d'oeuvre* of English novels read "Jorrocks".'

January 13th.

A little English telephonist who came to mend our apparatus said to me, 'Telephones are like women, sir. No one really knows anything about them. One fine day, something goes wrong; you try to find out why, no good, you swear, you shake them up a bit and all is well.'

January 14th.

At dinner an Irish colonel remarked:

'I am very annoyed; during my last leave I rented a house for my family, and now my wife writes that it is haunted. The owners really ought to tell one these things.'

'Perhaps they did not know it,' said our indulgent colonel.

'They knew it very well. When my wife went to complain, they got very confused, and ended by owning up. One of their great-grandmothers has walked from the drawing-room to her old bedroom for the last hundred and fifty years. They tried to excuse themselves by saying she was perfectly harmless. That is possible and I am quite willing to believe it, but it is none the less annoying for my wife. Do you think I can cancel my lease?'

I here risked a sceptical remark, but the whole Mess jumped on me. Irish ghosts are scientific facts.

'But why do phantoms love Irish houses more than others?'

'Because,' said the Irish colonel, 'we are a very sensitive race and we enter into communication with them more easily.'

And he crushed me with technical arguments on wireless telegraphy.

January 15th.

The colonel, having found out this morning that a motor-ambulance was going into Ypres, took me with him. In front of the hospital we found ourselves wedged in by a terrible block of waggons under a fierce bombardment.

A horse with its carotid artery cut by a bit of shell, and only held up by the shafts, was writhing in agony close by us. The drivers were swearing. Nothing to do but wait patiently in our car, shaken by explosions.

'Dr Johnson was right,' said the colonel to me, 'Whoever wants to be a hero ought to drink brandy.'

Then, as a fresh explosion made the debris of the ruined town in front of us tremble, he said:

'Messiou, how many inhabitants were there in Ypres before the War?'

January 20th.

We are going to leave Hondezeele. The red-hats are

getting agitated and already one sees the cyclists passing, the natural advance-guard of our migrations.

We were beginning to love this country: the village and the brigade, so distrustful of one another a month ago, had become really quite affectionate. But the gods are jealous.

> Brigade to march—*tomorrow's sky*
> *Will see us on the move,*
> The drums and pipes will sing good-bye
> *To every light-o'-love.*
>
> *The Highlanders, their kilts a-swirl*
> *Like eddies on the sand,*
> *With steadfast hymn and fiery skirl,*
> *Must join the devil's band.*
>
> *When Victory unveils the sun,*
> *Cold earth shall shrine their faith,*
> *But every field and farm they won,*
> *Shall know their constant wraith.*
>
> *And in our Flemish villages . . .*

Interrupted by the arrival of our successors, the Canadians, regarded by Madame Lemaire and her little boy with great suspicion. *That* won't last long.

CHAPTER XV

A GREAT ATTACK

A great attack was in preparation; it was a terrible secret
jealously guarded by headquarters; but Aurelle was informed of it several days beforehand by the German
communiqué published in the *Times*, and by Madame
Lemaire's little boy, who advised him not to repeat it.

However, the division was soon ordered to occupy
one of the sectors in the attack. The padre, optimistic as
ever, already foresaw triumphant marches, but the
colonel gently reminded him that the objectives were
simply a ridge, which in peace-time would be called
'a slight undulation in the ground,' and two villages
already destroyed. The real object was to engage the
forces of the enemy, who were at that moment advancing
in Russia. But this information only redoubled the
enthusiasm of the padre.

'You can say what you like, sir; if we hold this ridge
they cannot hold out in the valley, and we shall break
through their line. As for the retreat of the Russians,
that's capital. The Boche gets farther from his base,
lengthens his lines of communications, and he's done.'

'He is not,' said the colonel, 'but he will be one day,
and that's all that matters.'

The evening of the offensive, Aurelle received orders
from the colonel to go and act as liaison officer between
the headquarters of the division and some French

batteries, which were reinforcing the British artillery in this sector. He wished the Lennox good luck and left them for a day.

He spent the night in the garden of the little château where the general was living. The bombardment thundered on without ceasing. Aurelle walked up and down the paths of this garden, which had been pretty, but was now honeycombed with trenches and dug-outs, while camouflaged huts covered the lawns.

Towards midnight, the rain, the classic rain of an offensive, began to fall in large drops. The interpreter took shelter in a shed with some chauffeurs and motor-cyclists. He always liked to find himself among this class of Englishmen with their strong language and simple minds. These, like the rest, were good fellows, careless, courageous and light-hearted. They hummed the latest music-hall airs from London, showed him photographs of their wives, sweethearts and babies, and asked him when the damned war would be over. They shared on this subject the perfect optimism of the padre.

One of them, a little, quick-witted electrician, asked Aurelle to explain the Alsatian question. And so he told them about Saverne, the march-past of the Strasburg students before Kléber's statue, the pilgrimages of the Alsatians to Belfort for the 14th of July Review, and about the young men who at the age of twenty left family and fortune to go to France and become soldiers.

They told him that they could understand anyone loving France: it was a fine country. All the same there were not enough hedges in the landscape. But they appreciated the thrifty qualities of the women, the trees along the road, and the out-of-door cafés. They talked with enthusiasm about Verdun, but many of them had only grasped the idea of the Entente through Carpentier's victory in London.

The day dawned; the rain was now falling in torrents; on the lawn, the grass and soil was trodden into a sticky mass. Aurelle went up to the château; he met an aide-de-camp whom he knew and explained his orders.

'Oh yes,' he was told. 'I arranged that myself with the French liaison officer. If the telephone from the batteries happens to get cut, we shall have recourse to you. Go into the signalling room and sit down. In ten minutes from now,' he added, 'our men go over the top.'

The signalling room was the old winter garden. On the wall, a large-scale map of the trenches showed the British lines in black, and those of the enemy in red. At two long tables six telephone operators were installed. Silent officers with red tabs paced calmly up and down the room, and Aurelle thought of one of Major Parker's favourite remarks: 'A gentleman is never in a hurry.'

As five o'clock struck, the general came in and the officers stood still and said all together:

'Good morning, sir.'

'Good morning,' said the general politely.

He was very tall; his carefully brushed grey hair, neatly parted, framed his fine features. Gold lace shone on the red facings of his well-cut tunic.

Discovering Aurelle in his corner, he very kindly gave him a little 'Good morning' all to himself, and then he walked slowly, with his hands behind his back, between the two long tables of the telephonists. The noise of the guns had suddenly ceased, and nothing was heard in the room but the authoritative and measured step of the general.

A muffled bell tingled; an operator quietly made a note of the message on a pink form.

'5.5. a.m.,' read the general softly, '10th Brigade. Attack begun, enemy barrage not very effective, violent machine-gun fire.'

Then he passed the telegram to an officer, who stuck it on a long pin.

'Transmit it to the corps,' said the general.

And the officer wrote on a white paper: '5.10 a.m. 10th Brigade reports as follows: Attack begun. Enemy barrage not very effective. Violent machine-gun fire.'

He filed a carbon copy on another pin, and handed the original to an operator, who, in his turn, read it into the machine.

Inflexibly and monotonously the white and pink messages slowly accumulated. One brigade was in the enemy's first line trenches, the other had stopped before a concreted nest of machine-guns. The general reinforced them with details from the 3rd Brigade, then rang up the artillery several times to tell them to destroy the pill box. And these orders were transcribed on to the pink and white forms. An officer, standing before the huge map, carefully manoeuvred small coloured flags, and all this methodical agitation reminded Aurelle of a large banking house on the Stock Exchange.

Towards six o'clock in the morning, a Staff officer beckoned to him, and, leading him up to the map, showed him the emplacement of a French ·155 and asked him to go and see the officer, and tell him to destroy at all costs a certain railway cutting in which one or two enemy machine-guns were still firing. The telephone was no longer working.

Outside everything was calm; it was raining and the road was a river of yellow mud. The noise of the guns seemed farther off, but it was only an illusion, because one could see the wicked red light of the shells as they burst over the village in front of the house.

A few wounded, in hasty field-dressings, bleeding and muddy, were coming slowly up to the ambulance in small groups. Aurelle entered a little fir wood; the wet pine-needles seemed delightful walking after the mud. He heard the guns of the French battery quite close, but could not find it. He had been told: 'North-east corner of the wood.' But where the devil was the north-east? All at once a blue uniform moved among the trees. At the same moment a gun went off quite close to him, and, turning to the right, he saw the gunners on the edge of the wood well hidden by some thick bushes. A sergeant-major, astride a chair, tunic undone, *képi* pushed back, was in command. The men served the gun cleverly and without hurrying, like skilled workmen. One might have thought it a peaceful, open-air factory.

'Sir,' said one of the men, 'here is an interpreter.'

'Ah, now, perhaps, we shall find out why we can't get an answer from the English,' said the sergeant-major.

Aurelle gave him the orders, as the captain was at the observation post, and the lieutenant trying to repair the telephone.

'Right,' said the sergeant-major, a native of Lorraine with a quiet, sing-song voice. 'We will demolish it for you, young man.'

He telephoned to the captain; then, having found the cutting on the map, began his calculations. Aurelle stayed a few moments, glad to find this corner of the battlefield with no false romance, and also to hear French spoken again at last.

Then he took the path back to the château. Cutting across a meadow to find the high road, he approached the battlefield. A brigade of reinforcements was going up in line; he passed it in a contrary direction, with a few wounded to whom he offered a little brandy. The men who were going up to fight looked at the wounded in silence.

A shell whistled above the column; the heads bent like poplars in a wind. The shell burst in a deserted field. Then Aurelle, having passed the brigade, found himself on the road with the informal procession of wounded men. They had fever, they were dirty, they were bloody; but, thankful to be out of it, they hurried at the best pace they could muster towards the haven of white beds.

A party of German prisoners passed, guarded by a few Highlanders. Their terrified eyes, like those of trained animals, seemed to be looking for officers to salute.

As Aurelle arrived at the house, he saw two men in front of him carrying an officer on a stretcher. The officer evidently had some terrible wound, for his body was covered with dressings through which the blood had soaked, and was dripping slowly on to the muddy road.

'Yes, Aurelle, it's I,' said the dying man in a strange voice, and Aurelle recognized Captain Warburton. His good-looking merry face had become grave. 'O'Grady will not send me to the Duchess' hospital this time, messiou,' he gasped painfully. 'Will you say good-bye to the colonel for me—and let him write home that I did not suffer much. Hope that won't bother you. Thanks very much indeed.'

Aurelle, without being able to get out a word, pressed the hand of this maimed boy who had been so fond of War, and the stretcher-bearers carried him gently away.

On arriving at the château he found every one as calm as ever, but very serious. He gave in a report of his mission to the Staff officer, who thanked him absently.

'How is it going?' he asked an operator in a low voice.

'All right,' growled the man. 'All objectives attained, but the general killed. Would go himself to see why the Second Brigade did not come up—a shell buried him with Major Hall.'

Aurelle thought of the grey, smooth hair and fine features of the general, the gold and scarlet of his facings all soiled by the ignoble mud of battles. So much easy dignity, he thought, so much courteous authority, and tomorrow carrion, which the soldiers will trample under foot without knowing. But already, all round him, they were anxiously discussing who would be his successor.

In the evening, he went over to the Lennox with the regiment that was going to relieve them. The first person he saw was the doctor, who was working in a dug-out.

'I don't think the regiment did badly,' he said. 'I have not seen the colonel yet, but all the men tell me he was a marvel of courage and presence of mind. It appears, messiou, that we have the record number of Germans killed by one man. Private Kemble bayoneted twenty-four. Not bad, is it?'

'No,' said Aurelle, 'but it's horrible. Have you looked at Warburton, doctor? I met him on the road and he seemed very bad.'

'Done for,' said the doctor. 'And his friend Gibbons died here this afternoon, both legs blown off.'

'Oh, Gibbons too. Poor Gibbons! Do you remember, doctor, his talking about his plump little wife? No doubt at this very moment she is playing tennis with her sisters in some lovely English garden. And the bleeding limbs of her husband are there, in that blanket. It's terrible, doctor, all this.'

'Pooh!' answered the doctor, going to wash his hands, which were covered with blood. 'In three months you will see her portrait in the *Tatler*: "The beautiful widow of Captain Gibbons, M.C., who is shortly to be married to——" '

CHAPTER XVI

CHANSON DU COMTE DE DORSET
(1665)

Certes, just now, dear ladies, some
  Curled juvenile, your deary,
Is but too apt that song to hum
  Of which ye never weary—

Fa, do, sol, re.

The while he smoothes each glist'ning tress,
  With studied grace and air he,
With amorous glance and soft address,
  Is seeking to ensnare ye.

Fa, do, sol, re.

Meanwhile our battered vessel rocks
  To wild wave-music eerie,
And whistling wind our sort bemocks
With doleful Miserere.

Fa, do, sol, re.

Vainly, to chase the vision pale
  Of Fate that needs no query,
We crouch behind our bulwarks frail
  And croon in chorus dreary.

Fa, do, sol, re.

CHANSON DU COMTE DE DORSET

Devoted to the' infernal shades
*   By ladies' light vagary,*
The dismalest refrain invades
*   Our hearts in sad quandary.*

                    Fa, do, sol, re.

How now! Are ye so slight of soul,
*   Of love are ye so chary,*
Already you forget the rôle,
*   The text we never vary?*

                    Fa, do, sol, re.

Bethink you of those Roman dames
*   In household virtue wary,*
And, spinning wool, invoke the names
*   Of Powers tutelary.*

                    Fa, do, sol, re.

Can ye not, then, be such as they?
*   O hearken to the prayer he*
Intones, your lover far away,
*   And ill-content to share ye!*

                    Fa, do, sol, re.

For if inconstant you should prove,
*   With wave and weather veer ye,*
Beware lest this soft song of love
*   Should turn to* Dies Irae.

                    Fa, do, sol, re.

[99]

CHAPTER XVII

ANTS IN KHAKI

―――――――

The Lennox Highlanders, when the brigade was relieved, were sent for six days to a muddy field near Dickebusch. Dr O'Grady and Aurelle shared a tent, and dined together, the first evening, at the inn of the *Trois Amis*.

On their return, the stars shone brightly in a dark blue velvet sky. The soft moonlight lay on the grass of the meadows. A few tents in which a light was burning resembled great white lanterns; round the bivouac fires, blown about by the wind, the men sat swearing and singing.

'War makes light of time,' said the doctor, 'it is eternal and unalterable. This camp might be Caesar's, the Tommies round their fires, talking of their wives and their dangers, their boots and their horses, like the legionaries of Fabius or the veterans of the Grand Army. And, as in those days, on the other side of the hill, repose the barbarous Germans by their unyoked chariots.'

The burgundy of the *Trois Amis* inspired the doctor to hold forth like this.

'This tent is six thousand years old,' he said, 'it belongs to the warlike Bedouins who founded the empires of Babylon and Carthage. The restlessness of the ancient migrating people inspired them with a longing for the desert every year, and sent them forth from the city walls on profitable raids. It is this same force, Aurelle, which each summer, before the war, covered the deserted shores of Europe with nomadic tents, and it is the dim recollection of ancestral raids which, on August 1, 1914—holiday time, Aurelle, the time of migrations—incited the youngest of the barbarians to let loose their Emperor on the world. It is an old comedy which has been played for two thousand years, but the public still seem to take an interest in it. It is because there is always a fresh audience.'

'You are pessimistic this evening,' said Aurelle.

'What do you call pessimism?' said the doctor, painfully pulling off his stiff boots. 'I think that men will always have passions, and that they will never cease to go for one another at regular intervals with the most energetic means which the science of their time can procure for them, and the best chosen weapons with which to break each other's bones. I think that one sex will always try to please the other, and that from this elementary desire will eternally be born the need to vanquish rivals. With this object, nightingales, grasshoppers, prima donnas and statesmen will make use of their voices; peacocks, niggers and soldiers, of bright colours; rats, deer, tortoises and kings will go on fighting. All that is not pessimism, it is natural history!'

While talking the doctor had got into his sleeping-bag, and had seized a little book from a shelf made out of a biscuit box.

'Listen to this, Aurelle,' said he, 'and guess who wrote it.

' "My regrets about the War are unceasing, and I shall consent to admire your invincible general when I see the fight ended under honourable conditions. It is true that the brilliant successes which are your delight are also mine, because these victories, if we would use fortune wisely, will procure for us an advantageous peace. But if we let the moment pass when we might appear to give peace rather than receive it, I much fear that this splendid achievement will vanish in smoke. And if fate sends us reverses I tremble to think of the peace which will be imposed on the conquered by an enemy who has the courage to refuse it to the conquerors." '

'I don't know,' said Aurelle, yawning. 'Maximilian Harden ?'

'Senator Hanno at the Senate of Carthage,' said the doctor triumphantly. 'And in two thousand three hundred years some negro doctor, finding after the Great African War a speech by Lloyd George, will say, "These old sayings are sometimes very true." Your formidable European War is about as important, Aurelle, as the fights between two ant-heaps in the corner of my garden in Ireland.'

'It is much more than that to us,' said Aurelle, 'and it appears to me that the sort of sentiments it gives rise to are not animal. Do you think that ants are patriotic ?'

'Most certainly,' replied the doctor, 'the ants must be extremely patriotic. With them the warriors are highly fed by a race of servitors. Every season their armies set out to steal the eggs of the weaker species. Workers are hatched from them, born slaves in a foreign country. The military citizens are thus delivered from the slavery of work and these soldiers cannot even feed themselves. Shut up with honey, and without their nurse-slaves, they die of hunger. That is what is called civil mobilization. And if this war lasts long enough, one day, Aurelle, you will see a new human species appear: soldier-men. They will be born with helmets and armour, impervious to bullets and provided with natural weapons; the Suffragettes will be the sexless slaves who will feed these warriors, while a few queens will, in special institutions, bring national infants into the world.'

Thus discoursed the doctor, in the friendly silence of the camp by the soft light of the moon; and Aurelle, who had gone to sleep, saw visions of enormous ants in khaki marching by, commanded by the little doctor.

CHAPTER XVIII

'TRANSMITTED
TO THE PROPER QUARTER'

The orderlies brought the rum, sugar, and boiling water. The padre began patience, the colonel played 'Destiny Waltz', and Dr O'Grady, who in times of peace was doctor at an asylum, talked about lunatics.

'I had the care of a rich American who thought he was surrounded by a belt of poisoned gas,' he said. 'In order to save his life, he had a special bed made for himself surrounded by a cage of white wood. He passed his days in this safe shelter, dressed in nothing but a red bathing suit, writing a book in twenty thousand chapters on the life and works of Adam. His room had a triple door on which he had carved, "Gas carriers are warned that there are wolf-traps inside." He sent for me every day, and when I went in he always said, "I have never seen any creatures so stupid, so wicked, so rotten, or so dense as English doctors." '

' "I have never seen," ' repeated the padre with great satisfaction, ' "any creatures so stupid, so wicked, or so dense as English doctors." '

'Upon which,' continued the doctor, 'he turned his back on me, and, clothed in his red bathing suit, set to work again at the twenty-thousandth chapter on the works of Adam.'

'Here, messiou,' interrupted the colonel, who was

[104]

examining some official papers, 'is some work for you,' and he passed over to Aurelle a thick bundle of papers covered with multi-coloured seals.

It commenced thus:

'From the Stationmaster at B—— to the Military Superintendent of the Station at B——

'I have the honour to inform you that Mademoiselle Héninghem, gate-keeper at Hondezeele, complains of the following facts: the English soldiers camped along the railway line are in the habit of performing their ablutions in the open air, which is a shocking sight for the lady in question, who, from the nature of her work, cannot avoid seeing them. I shall be obliged if you will give orders that this regrettable state of affairs shall be put a stop to as soon as possible.'

(Signature.)

(Seal.)

'From the Military Superintendent of the Station at B—— to the Superintendent W——

'Transmitted to the proper quarter.'

(Signed.)

(Seal.)

'The Superintendent W—— to the D.A.D.R.T.

'I shall be obliged if you will give orders that the camp in question be surrounded with a fence of sufficient thickness to render the visibility at fifty yards' distance practically nil.'

'That last man,' said Aurelle, 'is a polytechnician.'
The padre asked what that was.

'A polytechnician is a man who believes that all beings, alive or dead, can be precisely defined and submitted to an algebraic calculation. A polytechnician puts on the same plane victory a tempest, and love. I knew one who, commanding a fortress and having to draw up some orders in case of aerial attack, began thus: "The Fortress of X—— will be attacked by an aerial engine when a vertical line from the engine to the earth finds the centre of the fortification," and so on.'

'Do not abuse the Polytechnic, Aurelle,' said the doctor. 'It is the most original of your institutions and the best. The personal cult of Napoleon is so well preserved that each year France presents two hundred Lieutenant Bonapartes to the astonished Government.'

'Go on translating, messiou,' said the colonel.

'D.A.D.R.T. to the Superintendent.

'This does not concern me but a division that is resting. You must address your claim to the A.G. by the intermediary of the French Mission.'

(Signed.)

(Seal.)

'Superintendent —— to the Base Commandant G.H.Q.

'I have the honour to forward herewith, for any action you consider necessary, a Memorandum concerning a complaint from Mademoiselle Héninghem of Honde-zeele.'

(Signed.)

(Seal.)

And so it went on: Base Commandant to the French

Mission; French Mission to the Adjutant-General; A. G. to the Army; Army to the Corps; Division to the Brigade; Brigade to the Colonel of the Lennox Highlanders. And it was signed with illustrious names, Colonel, Chief Staff Officer for the General, Brigadier, Major-General; thus the modest scruples of Mademoiselle Héninghem of Hondezeele were clothed, in the course of a long journey, with purple, gold and glory.

'This is a tiresome business,' said Colonel Bramble solemnly. 'Parker, answer it, will you, like a good chap.'

The major wrote for several minutes, then read out:

'This regiment having left the Camp at Hondezeele two months and a half ago, it is unfortunately impossible to take the measures desired in the matter. Moreover, having ascertained the great cost of a fence of sufficient height, I beg to suggest that it would be more advantageous to the allied Governments to replace the gatekeeper at Hondezeele by a person of mature age and proved experience, to whom the spectacle described herewith would be inoffensive and even agreeable.'

'No, Parker, no,' said the colonel firmly, 'I shall not sign that. Give me a piece of paper. I will answer myself.'

He wrote simply:

'Noted and returned.
BRAMBLE,
Colonel.'

'You are a wise man, sir,' said Parker.

'I know the game,' said the colonel. 'I have played it for thirty years.'

'Once upon a time,' said the doctor, 'there were two officers who, on the same day, each lost something belonging to His Majesty's Government. The first one mislaid a coal-bucket; the second a motor-lorry. Now you must know, Aurelle, that in our army an officer has to pay for anything which he may lose by negligence out of his own pocket. The two officers, therefore, received notices from the War Office advising one that he would have to pay three shillings, and the other that a thousand pounds would be stopped from his pay. The first wished to defend himself; he had never had any coal-buckets, and tried to prove it. He stopped his promotion, and in the end had to pay the three bob. The second, who knew a thing or two, just wrote at the bottom of the paper, "Noted and returned," and sent it back to the War Office. There, following an old and wise rule, a clerk lost the correspondence and the officer never heard anything more of *that* little matter.'

'That isn't a bad story, doctor,' said Major Parker; 'but in the case of the loss of property belonging to the Government there is a much better method than yours— Colonel Boulton's method.

'Colonel Boulton commanded an ammunition depot. He was responsible, among other things, for fifty machine-guns. One day he noticed that there were only forty-nine in the depot. All the inquiries, and punishment of the sentries, failed to restore the missing machine-gun.

'Colonel Boulton was an old fox and had never acknowledged himself in the wrong. He simply mentioned in his monthly return that the tripod of a machine-gun had been broken. They sent him a tripod to replace the other without any comment.

'A month later, on some pretext or other, he reported the sighting apparatus of a machine-gun as out of order;

the following month he asked for three screw-nuts; then a recoil plate, and bit by bit in two years he entirely destroyed his machine-gun. And correspondingly, bit by bit, the Army Ordnance Department reconstructed it for him without attaching any importance to the requisitions for the separate pieces.

'Then Colonel Boulton, satisfied at last, inspected his machine-guns, and found fifty-one.

'While he had been patiently reconstructing the lost gun, some damned idiot had found it in a corner. And Boulton had to spend two years of clever manipulation of his books to account for the new gun which had been evolved out of nothing.'

'Messiou,' said the colonel, 'do you remember the gate-keeper at Hondezeele? I should not have thought it of her.'

'No more should I,' said Aurelle. 'She was very pretty.'

'Messiou!' said the padre.

CHAPTER XIX

A MIRACULOUS CURE

'Doctor,' said the padre, 'give me a cigar.'

'Are you aware, padre, that my cigars were rolled on the bare thighs of the young girls of Havana?'

'O'Grady,' said the colonel severely, 'I consider that remark out of place.'

'Give me one all the same,' said the padre. 'I must smoke a cigar to help me find a text for my sermon. The quarter-master made me promise to go and see the motor-drivers who are at the back, and I don't know what to talk to them about.'

'Look here, padre, I will give you an appropriate text; lend me your Bible a moment. Ah, here it is. Listen! "But David said, Ye shall not do so, my brethren, with that which the Lord hath given us . . . but as his part is that goeth down to the battle, so shall his part be that tarrieth by the stuff; they shall part alike." '

'Admirable,' said the padre, 'admirable! But tell me, O'Grady, how is it that an old sinner like you knows the Holy Scriptures so well?'

'I studied the Book of Samuel a good deal from an asylum doctor's point of view,' said the doctor. 'Saul's neurasthenia interested me. His attacks are very well described. I have also diagnosed the madness of Nebuchadnezzar. They were two very different types. Saul was apathetic and Nebuchadnezzar violent.'

'I wish you would leave Nebuchadnezzar alone,' said the colonel.

'I am very much afraid of asylum doctors,' said Major Parker. 'Violent, depressed, or apathetic, we are all mad, according to them.'

'What do you call mad?' said the doctor. 'I certainly can see in you, and in the colonel, and Aurelle, all the phenomena which I observed in the asylum.'

'Ugh!' said the colonel, horrified.

'But I do, sir. Between Aurelle, who forgets the war by reading Tolstoy, and some of my old friends who thought they were Napoleon or Mahomet, there is a difference in degree but not in nature. Aurelle browses on novels from a morbid desire to live the life of someone else; my patients substitute for their miserable life that of some great personage whose history they have read and whose lot they envy.

'Oh, I know your objections, Aurelle. You know, all the time you are dreaming of the loves of Prince Bolkonsky, that you are the Interpreter Aurelle, attached to the Lennox Highlanders, but when Queen Elizabeth is scrubbing the floor of my office, she does not know that she is Mrs Jones, charwoman, of Hammersmith. But incoherence is not the monopoly of madness: all the main ideas of a sane man are irrational erections built up, for better or worse, to express his deepest feelings.'

'Parker,' said the colonel, 'can you think of anything to stop him?'

'A No. 5 grenade, sir,' said the major.

But the doctor went on imperturbably:

'One of my patients was a country gentleman, who after being a model of piety for the first part of his life suddenly became an atheist. He gave carefully thought out reasons for it, and discoursed with a good deal of erudition on questions of doctrine, but the only true cause of his conversion to the wrong side was because his wife ran away with the clergyman of his village. Oh, I beg your pardon, padre, you don't mind, do you?'

'I? I have not been listening to you for ages,' said the padre, who was dealing out patience.

'It is just the same thing,' continued the doctor, turning to the docile Aurelle, 'with a man who is too refined for the class in which chance has placed him. At first he is simply jealous and unhappy. Influenced by these feelings, he becomes violently critical of society in order to account for his hate and disappointment.

'Nietzsche was a genius because he delighted in persecution. Karl Marx was a dangerous maniac. It is only when the feelings of discontent which he tries to explain coincide with those of a whole class, or a whole nation, that the impassioned theorist becomes a prophet, or a hero; while, if he confines himself to explaining that he would rather have been born an Emperor, they shut him up.'

'Moral,' said the major, 'shut up all theorists.'

'And the doctor,' said the colonel.

'No, not all,' said the doctor. 'We treat the subject just as the ancients did. All primitive people thought that a lunatic was possessed by a spirit. When his incoherent words more or less accord with the moral prejudices of the time, the spirit is a good one, and the man is a saint. In the opposite case, the spirit is evil and the man must be suppressed. It is just according to the time and place and the doctors, whether a prophetess would be worshipped as a priestess or ducked as a witch. Innumerable violent lunatics have escaped the cells, thanks to the War, and their very violence has made heroes of them. And in every Parliament there are at least five or six undisputed idiots who got elected for their madness, through the admiration of their constituents.'

'Say five or six hundred,' said Major Parker, 'and it will be the first sensible thing you have said tonight.'

'That's because my madness agrees with yours on that subject,' said the doctor.

'Doctor,' said the colonel, 'you understand treatment by suggestion, don't you? I wish you would calm down your hospital sergeant a bit. He is so nervous that he begins to tremble and becomes perfectly speechless if I speak to him. I really believe I terrify him. See what you can do, like a good fellow.'

Next morning, Dr O'Grady sent for Sergeant Freshwater to his tent and talked kindly to him.

Freshwater, a lean Albino with heavy, stupid eyes, owned that he lost his head whenever the colonel came near him.

'Well, my friend,' said the doctor, 'we will cure you of that in five minutes. Sit down there.'

He made some passes to create an atmosphere favourable to suggestion, then began:

'You are not afraid of the colonel, you know he is a man just like you and me—you rather like talking to him. Look closely at his face when he speaks to you. His moustache is always cut a little too short on the left side.'

The doctor went on like this for a quarter of an hour describing the rugged features and funny ways of the colonel, then sent away the sergeant, telling him that he was cured, and not to forget it the first time he met his commanding officer.

[113]

A few hours later, Colonel Bramble, going out for his lunch, met the hospital sergeant on one of the duckboards used for going through the camp. Freshwater stepped on one side, saluted, and began to laugh silently.

'Whatever is the matter, sergeant ?' said the astonished colonel.

'Oh, sir,' replied Freshwater in fits of laughter, 'I cannot help laughing when I look at you, you have such a funny face!'

The colonel, in a few well-chosen words, destroyed the doctor's learned suggestions for ever; then, establishing himself in front of the tinned lobster, he complimented O'Grady on his miraculous cure.

'I have never seen,' said the padre, 'any creatures so stupid, so wicked, so rotten, or so dense as English doctors.'

'Medicine is a very old joke,' said Major Parker, 'but it still goes on. Now, doctor tell the truth, for once: what do you know more than we do about illnesses and their remedies ?'

'That's right,' said the padre, 'attack his religion; he often attacks mine.'

'When I was in India,' said the colonel, 'an old army doctor gave me for every malady the remedy which just suited me. For palpitations of the heart, a large glass of brandy; for insomnia, three or four glasses of port after dinner; for stomachic disorders, a bottle of dry champagne at each meal. And, as long as one was feeling well, whisky and soda.'

'Excellent, sir,' said Aurelle. 'Before the War I drank nothing but water and I was always ill; since I have been with you I have adopted whisky and I feel much better.'

'Yes, you look it,' said the colonel. 'I had a friend,

Major Fetherstonhaugh, who began to have fits of dizziness when he was about forty; he went to see a doctor who thought it was the whisky and advised him to drink milk for a time; well, in ten days he was dead.'

'And a good thing too,' said the padre.

'But I expect——' began the doctor.

'Happy are those who expect nothing,' said the padre, 'for they shall not be disappointed.'

'What, you too, padre!' said the doctor. 'Take care; if you ruin doctors by your malevolent remarks, I shall found a society for the exportation to the Colonies of mechanical idols and ovens for cooking missionaries.'

'That is an excellent idea,' said the padre. 'I must see about it.'

CHAPTER XX

A PAUSE IN THE CONVERSATION

The brigade, kept in reserve for the division, was ordered to go and camp at H——. As a dentist measures the extent of a cavity at a glance, the men of the Lennox, expert in bombardments, cast a professional eye over the village. Round the château and the church it was done for: houses in ruins, pavements torn up, trees smashed. The weaving factory had been badly damaged. The rest was not so unhealthy, a little knocked about, perhaps, but habitable.

The house where Colonel Bramble had established his Mess had already been hit by a shell. It had burst in the garden, breaking the window-panes and marking the walls. Madame, a dear little old lady, made light of these blemishes, which had depreciated her house in value.

'Oh, just a shell, *monsieur l'officier !*' she said. 'Quite a small shell; I put the base of it there on my mantelpiece. It's nothing, as you can see. True, they make a mess of everything, but I am not afraid of them!'

The colonel asked her how many windows had been broken.

'I don't like this house,' said the padre, as they sat down to dinner.

'The life of a soldier,' replied the colonel, 'is one of great hardship, not infrequently mingled with moments of real danger.'

'Be not dismayed, padre,' said the doctor. 'Shells fall like drops of water: if it rains much the whole pavement gets wet.'

'The Lennox Mess has always been lucky,' said Major Parker.

'Luck is nothing,' said the doctor.

'One can see you are not a gambler,' remarked Aurelle.

'One can see that you are not a mathematician,' said the doctor.

The padre expostulated:

'What? Luck nothing? How about little Taylor, killed by a shell in Poperinghe Station at the very moment that he was arriving at the front line for the first time! You don't call that bad luck?'

'Not more than if an old habitué like me was wiped out by a whizz-bang, padre. You are astonished at Taylor being killed the first minute, just as you would be surprised if, in a lottery of a million tickets, Number One should win, although that number had obviously as much chance as, say, 327,645. Some one must be the last man killed in this war, but you will see that his family will not think it ordinary.'

'You are a fanatic, O'Grady,' said Parker, 'you must have an explanation for everything; there are more things in heaven and earth than are dreamed of in your philosophy. I believe, myself, in good luck and bad luck because I have noticed it: I believe in presentiments because I have had them, and events have confirmed them. When I was being sent home, after the Transvaal War, I got an order to embark on a certain ship. Well, two days before it started I suddenly had a presentiment that I must avoid sailing in that ship at all costs. I went sick and waited a fortnight longer. The transport I missed was completely lost and no one ever knew how. Then again, why are you so certain, doctor, that aspirin will cure your headache? Because aspirin has cured it before. Where's the difference?'

'The major is right,' said Aurelle. 'To say that you do not believe in a man's bad luck because you cannot find it at his autopsy, is like saying that the tuner has taken the piano to pieces, and therefore Mozart had no soul.'

The quartermaster, who was dining with them that evening, threw his weight into discussion:

'There *are* things that cannot be explained, doctor. For instance, I hit you in the face: you shut your eye—why?'

There was an astounded silence.

'Another instance,' remarked the padre at last. 'Why is it that if there is a pause in the conversation, it is always twenty minutes to, or twenty minutes past, the hour?'

'But that's not true,' said the doctor.

'It was true this time, anyhow,' said Aurelle, looking at his watch.

'It may be once or twice,' said the doctor irritably, 'but it cannot always happen.'

'All right, doctor, all right,' said the padre. 'You notice it for several days and I think you will change your mind.'

The colonel said:

'My men tell me that if a shell falls on a dug-out where there are gunners and infantry, the latter are killed and the gunners are spared. Why?'

'But it is not true, sir.'

'And why must one never light three cigarettes with the same match?'

'But you may, sir, it does not matter a bit.'

'Ah, there I disagree with you, doctor,' said the colonel. 'I am not superstitious, but I would not do that for anything in the world.'

'Why do people dressed in green always lose at Monte Carlo?' said Aurelle.

'But it is not true!' roared the doctor, exasperated.

'It is easy to argue like you,' said Parker. 'Everything you do not agree with is not true.'

'There are,' said the padre, 'no creatures so wicked and so dense as English doctors.'

'Messiou,' said the colonel, 'are the gunners equally lucky in the French Army?'

'I have often remarked it,' said Aurelle, who liked Colonel Bramble very much.

The colonel therefore triumphed, and tried to put an end to the discussion, which bored him.

'I am so very sorry,' he said, 'I cannot give you the gramophone tonight. I have no more needles.'

'That *is* a pity,' said the padre.

The window-panes shook; a big gun went off close to the house. Aurelle went to the window and saw behind a farm, silhouetted in black against the orange twilight of the sky, a yellowish smoke, slowly dispersing.

'There's the old man beginning to strafe again,' said the padre. 'I don't like this house.'

'You will have to put up with it, padre; the Staff captain won't give us another; he's a boy who knows his own mind.'

'Yes,' said the colonel, 'he is a very nice boy too; he is one of Lord Bamford's sons.'

'His father, the old Lord, was a fine rider,' said Parker.

'His sister,' replied the colonel, 'married a cousin of Graham, who was a major in our first battalion at the beginning of the War, and is now a brigadier-general.'

Aurelle, foreseeing that such an interesting subject, so rich in the possibility of unexpected developments, would occupy the entire evening, tried to scribble some verses, still meditating on luck and chance.

> *'Pascal, thou said'st if Cleopatra's nose*
> *Had shorter been, we were not—where we are . . .'*

A new and formidable detonation put a subtle rhyme out of his head; discouraged, he tried another:

> *'I trust you will not look askance*
> *For once I deal in platitude;*
> *Tonight, to laws of luck and chance*
> *The Mess defines its attitude.'*

Another shell fell so close that the colonel got up suddenly.

'They are beginning to bombard the château again,' he said. 'I am going to see where that one fell.'

Major Parker and the doctor followed him into the street, but Aurelle, who was again rhyming, stayed with the padre, who had just begun the same patience for the fourteenth time that evening. The three officers had gone about a hundred yards when another explosion took place behind them.

'That one was not far from the Mess,' said the doctor. 'I am going to tell Madame to go down into the cellar.'

He retraced his steps and found a new shell-hole in

front of the house. The house seemed all right; through the broken window the doctor saw the padre and called out to him:

'A near thing that time, padre. Are you all right? Where is Aurelle?'

But the padre did not move: with his head leaning on his arms crossed over the scattered cards, he appeared to be gazing vaguely at the doctor, who entered at a bound and touched the padre on the shoulder.

He was dead. A piece of shell had entered his temple, which was bleeding slowly. Aurelle had fallen on the floor. He was unconscious and covered with blood, but the doctor, bending over him, found that he still breathed. As he was unfastening his tunic and shirt, the colonel and Parker arrived with their measured tread and stopped abruptly at the door.

'The padre has been killed, sir,' said the doctor simply. 'Aurelle is hit, too, but I don't think it is serious. No, it's his shoulder—nothing much.'

The colonel groaned sympathetically.

Parker helped O'Grady to lay the Frenchman on a table; a crumpled piece of paper attracted the colonel's attention; he picked it up and read with difficulty:

> '*Why must you ever close my eyes*
> *Before you kiss my lips?*'

'What is it all about?' he said.

'It belongs to Aurelle,' said the doctor.

The colonel carefully folded the little sheet of paper and slid it respectfully into the young Frenchman's pocket. Then, after the doctor had finished dressing the wound and had sent for an ambulance, they laid the padre on Madame's humble bed. They all took their hats off and stood silent for some time contemplating the strangely softened features of the childlike old man.

The doctor looked at his watch; it was twenty minutes past nine.

CHAPTER XXI

LONG LIVE WHOEVER-IT-IS!

Aurelle, on leaving hospital, was attached, while convalescent, to the English colonel, Musgrave, who commanded a supply depot at Estrées, a little village well behind the line. He missed the evenings with the Lennox Mess, but buying fodder and wood took him some way out into the pretty undulating country with its clear streams, and he loved Estrées, hiding its innumerable belfries among the flowery hills.

It was a very antique city, and in its youth, in the time of the *seigneurs* of Estrées, had played an important part in the affairs of France. For several hundred years she had defended her ramparts against the troops of the Kings of England, and from her walls she could see those same soldiers today camped about her, this time as familiar and courteous guests. Her tenacious burghers had repulsed both Leaguers and Spaniards with equal success. She now slept in smiling old age, having seen too many things to be surprised any more, while still retaining from the times of her glory her casket of beautiful mansions, built among courts and gardens with the noble simplicity of line dating from the best periods.

Colonel Musgrave and his officers inhabited the large and handsome house of the Dutch merchant, Van Mopez, whom Colbert had established at Estrées to introduce the art of weaving and dyeing cloth. Aurelle liked to go and sit in the garden and read a History of Estrées written by Monsieur Jean Valines, correspondence member of the Amiens Academy, and author of 'Nouvelles observations sur les miracles de la chapelle d'Estrées.'

This excellent work contained accounts of the great rejoicings and high festivals with which Estrées the Faithful had received the Kings, when they came to kneel and worship at the feet of the miraculous image in the chapel of St Ferréol.

The municipal worthies, between the royal visits, prudently and carefully preserved the white and blue draperies embroidered with fleurs-de-lis, and the decorations of painted scenery.

The Revolution had rather upset these domestic arrangements; the fleurs-de-lis had to be removed and a red fringe sewn along the blue and white draperies, so that the square of Saint-Ferréol could be decorated at a small cost for the fête of the Supreme Being. Aurelle loved the description:

'The cortège, preceded by music and drums, consisted first of a half-company of the National Guard carrying a banner on which was inscribed: "Up with the People, down with Tyrants."

'Then came the mothers of families carrying their infants in their arms; children of both sexes clothed in the most beautiful ornaments of their age—innocence and candour; young girls adorned with their charms and virtues; and the members of that Society so dreaded by traitors, in which were united the defenders of the truth, the upholders of public opinion, and the indefatigable guardians of the people.

'The whole cortège gathered at the foot of a mound erected in the square of Saint-Ferréol. There, the people

of Estrées swore fidelity to the laws of nature and
humanity, and subsequently a group of figures represent-
ing Despotism and Imposture were consumed by flames;
Wisdom arose out of the ashes and on his shield was
written: "I guard the Republic." '

Aurelle turned over some pages, very few, for, as
Monsieur Jean Valines said, the happy sterility of the
archives of Estrées during the Revolution recorded no
other facts worthy of notice than two fêtes, a fire, and a
flood. Next came the visit of the First Consul. He came
to Estrées accompanied by his wife and several general
officers, and was received by the authorities under a
triumphal arch, erected at the Saint-Ferréol Gate,
adorned with this inscription: 'The Grateful Inhabitants
of this City swear Allegiance and Fidelity to the Conqueror of Marengo.'

The Mayor presented the keys of the town on a silver
dish covered with bay leaves. 'I take them, *citoyen maire*,
and I return them to you,' replied Bonaparte.

'The National Guard lined the route and cries of
"Long live Bonaparte! Long live the First Consul!"
were repeated enthusiastically a thousand times. The
First Consul visited the Van Mopez factory and distributed a day's pay among the workmen. The day ended
with illuminations and a brilliant ball.

'A short time after his marriage with Marie-Louise,
Napoleon came back, accompanied by the Empress. The
square of Saint-Ferréol was a magnificent spectacle,
decorated with red and white draperies and garlands of
green leaves. A triumphal arch had been erected with
the inscription: "*Augusto Napoleoni Augustæque Mariæ
Ludovicæ Strataville semper fidelis.*" '

A few more pages further on and it was March, 1814;

for six days no couriers got through to Estrées from Paris, and then she heard of the fall of the Emperor.

'At three o'clock in the afternoon, the magistrates, assembled in the Town Hall, summoned the inhabitants with the ringing of bells. The Mayor appeared on the balcony of the large hall and proclaimed the allegiance of the town to the restored Bourbons. The spectators received this speech with oft-repeated cries of "Long live the King!" "Long live Louis XVIII!" and all put on the white cockade.

'The news soon came that Louis XVIII had landed at Calais and that he would pass through Estrées. A guard of honour was formed and a triumphal arch was erected at the Saint-Ferréol gate. It bore this inscription: *"Regibus usque suis urbs Stratavilla fidelis."*

'The clergy from every parish approached to compliment the King, and the Mayor presented the keys of the town on a silver dish adorned with fleurs-de-lis. The King replied, "Monsieur le maire, I take the flowers, and give you back the keys." Then the sailors and footmen unharnessed the horses from the carriage, and drew him themselves into the town. The excitement of the crowd was impossible to describe; every house was decorated with blue and white draperies and green garlands, mottoes and white flags, covered with fleurs-de-lis.

'The King was present at a *Te Deum* sung in Saint-Ferréol, and repaired, still drawn by sailors, to the Abbey of Saint-Pierre, where he was to lodge the night.'

The evening drew slowly in; the quaint, thick lettering of the old book was becoming indistinct, but Aurelle wanted to finish the melancholy history of these inconstant people. Skipping the triumphal entry of Charles X, he came to the July insurrection.

'On the 29th of July, 1830, there were no newspapers; but letters and a few travellers arriving from Paris announced that the tricolour flag had been hoisted on the towers of Notre-Dame. A few days later they learnt that the fighting had stopped, and that the heroic population of the capital remained in possession of all their outposts.

'Louis-Philippe, accompanied by the Dukes of Orleans and Nemours, soon after passed Estrées on his way to Lille. He was received under a triumphal arch by the Mayor and Corporation. Every house was hung with draperies in the three colours. An immense crowd filled the air with their acclamations. The King arrived at the square of Saint-Ferréol, where the National Guard and several companies of *douaniers* awaited him.

'The various corps of the urban guards in their best clothes; the strangeness of the rural guards, with a large number of Napoleon's old soldiers in their ranks with their original uniforms; the intrepid seamen of Cayeux carrying in triumph their fishing prizes, ten old tricolour banners; the sailors, with their carbines, bandoliers and cutlasses in their hands, all made the gayest of spectacles, and the picturesque fête delighted the King and the officers of his staff.'

There Jean Valines' book concluded, but Aurelle, while watching the garden fading slowly in the twilight, amused himself by imagining what followed. A visit from Lamartine, no doubt; then one from Napoleon III, the triumphal arches and inscriptions, and quite lately, perhaps, Carnot or Fallières receiving from the mayor, in the square of Saint-Ferréol, the assurance of the unalterable devotion of the faithful people of Estrées to the Republic. Then in the future: unknown governors, the decorations, perhaps red, perhaps blue, until the day when some blind god would come and crush with his heel this venerable human ant-hill.

'And each time,' he mused, 'the enthusiasm is sincere and the vows loyal, and these honest tradesmen rejoice to see passing through their ancient portals the new rulers, in the choice of whom they have had no part.

'Happy province! You quietly accept the Empires which Paris brings forth with pain, and the downfall of a government means no more to you than changing the words of a speech or the flowers on a silver dish. If Dr O'Grady were here he would quote Ecclesiastes to me.'

He tried to remember it:

'What profit hath a man of all his labour which he taketh under the sun?

'One generation passeth away, and another generation cometh; but the earth abideth for ever.

'The thing that hath been, it is that which shall be; and that which is done is that which shall be done; and there is no new thing under the sun.'

'Aurelle,' said Colonel Musgrave, who had quietly approached, 'if you want to see the bombardment after dinner, go up to the top of the hill. The sky is all lit up. We attack tomorrow morning.'

And a distant muffled thundering floated on the calm evening air. A melancholy and ancient peal of bells rang out from the Spanish belfry in the market-place. The first stars twinkled above the two ironical towers of the church of Saint-Ferréol and the proud old town fell asleep to the familiar sound of battle.

CHAPTER XXII

ANOTHER POEM

In the soft evening air the garden drowses;
'J'ai du bon tabac' thinly sounds afar;
The bells are chiming slow, and farther, rouses
The distant, instant, deepfelt voice of war.

One star stands out upon the darkling sky;
Against the west the tree-tops draw, outlined,
A woodcut, Japanese, the moon behind;
A voice, singing; dogs bark; the day is by.

Life seems so sweet, so calm the valley's mood,
That, did not bitter memories undeceive,
On such a night almost could one believe
This false world was of God—that God was good.

But even now, where the faint hills decline,
Under this very sky, now calm as when
Its peace was real—past that near confine,
The gates of hell yawn wide for living men.

CHAPTER XXIII

TO DO WITH GOATS

Colonel Musgrave was drinking his coffee in the hand-some *salon* of the merchant, Van Mopez; he opened a pink official telegram and read:

'Director of Commissariat to Colonel Musgrave. Marseilles Indian Depot overcrowded meet special train 1000 goats with native goatherds find suitable quarters and organize temporary farm.'

'Damn the goats!' he said.

His job being to feed Australians, he thought it hard that he had to bear in addition the consequences of the religious laws of the Hindoos. But nothing troubled Colonel Musgrave long; he sent for his interpreter.

'Aurelle,' he said, 'I am expecting a thousand goats this evening; you will take my motor and scour the country. I must have a suitable piece of ground in five hours and a small building for the shepherds. If the owner refuses to let you hire them, you will commandeer them. Have a cigar? Good-bye.'

Having thus disposed of this first anxiety, he turned to his adjutant.

'We now want an O.C. Goats!' he said. 'It will be an excellent reason for getting rid of Captain Cassell, who arrived yesterday. *Captain!* I asked him what he did in peace-time—musical critic of the *Morning Leader!*'

So that is how Captain Cassell, musical critic, was

promoted goatherd-in-chief. Aurelle found a farmer's wife whose husband had been called up, and he persuaded her, at the cost of much eloquence, that the presence of a thousand goats in her orchards would be the beginning of all sorts of prosperity. He went in the evening to the station with Cassell to fetch the goats, and they both passed through the town at the head of the picturesque flock, herded by ancient Indians, who looked exactly like the shepherds in the Bible.

Colonel Musgrave ordered Cassell to send him a hundred goats per day for the front. After the fourth day Cassell sent over a short note by one of the children from the farm, announcing, as if it were quite a natural thing, that his flock would be exhausted the next day and asking for another contingent of goats.

On opening this extraordinary missive, the colonel was so choked with rage that he forgot to proclaim, according to custom, that Cassell was a damned fool. The numbers were too simple for an error to be possible. Cassell had received one thousand goats; he had sent off four hundred, he ought to have six hundred left.

The colonel ordered his car and commanded Aurelle to take him to the farm. A pretty, deeply cut road led them there. The buildings were in the rustic, solid style of the end of the eighteenth century.

'It is a charming spot,' said the interpreter, proud of his find.

'Where is that damned fellow Cassell?' said the colonel.

They found him in the kitchen having a French lesson from the farmer's daughter. He got up with the easy grace of a rural gentleman whom friends from town had surprised in his hermitage.

'Hullo, colonel,' he said, 'I am very glad to see you.'

The colonel went straight to the point:

'What's this damned letter that you sent me this morning? You received a thousand goats; you sent me four hundred of them. Show me the others.'

The ground behind the farm sloped gently down to a wooded valley; it was planted with apple-trees. Near a stable, sitting in the mud, the Hindoo shepherds tasted prematurely the joys of Nirvana.

A horrible smell arose from the valley, and, coming nearer, the colonel saw about a hundred swollen and rotting carcases of goats scattered about the enclosure. A few thin kids dismally gnawed the bark of the apple-trees. In the distance, among the copses which covered the other side of the valley, one could see goats which had escaped browsing on the young trees. At this lamentable sight, Aurelle pitied the unfortunate Cassell.

The colonel maintained a hostile and dangerous silence.

'Isn't it beautiful, colonel,' said the musical critic with soft and stilted speech, 'to see all those little white spots among the green?'

'Could not one,' suggested Aurelle on the return journey, 'ask the advice of a competent man? Perhaps goats cannot stand sleeping out of doors in this damp climate, and perhaps also they are not being fed properly.'

The colonel frowned.

'In the South African war,' he said after a silence, 'we used a large number of oxen for our transport. One day these damned oxen started dying by hundreds, and no one knew why. Great excitement at headquarters. Some general found an expert, who, after boring the whole army with his questions, ended by declaring that the oxen were cold. He had noticed the same sickness in the north of India. There they protected the beasts by making them wear special clothing. Any normal individual with common sense could see that the oxen were simply overworked. But the report followed its course, and arrived at general headquarters, and from there they wired to India for a few thousand rugs for cattle.

'So far all went well, the oxen died as fast as ever, the well-paid expert had a damned good time—up to the arrival of the rugs. It is very easy to put clothing on an Indian cow who waits patiently with lowered head. But an African bullock—you try, and see what it's like. After several trials, our drivers refused to do it. They sent for the expert and said to him, "You asked for rugs for the beasts: here they are. Show us how to put them on." He was damned lucky to get out of hospital in six months.'

That same evening another pink telegram arrived from the Director of Commissariat:

'Goats arrive at the front half dead pray take steps that these animals may have some wish to live.'

Colonel Musgrave then decided to telegraph to Marseilles and ask for an expert on goats.

The expert arrived two days later, a fat farmer from the South, sergeant of Territorials. With the help of Aurelle, he had a long conversation with the colonel.

'There is one thing,' he said, 'that goats cannot get on without, and that is heat. You must make very low wooden sheds for them; without any openings; let them stew in their own juice, and they will be happy!'

He remarked to the interpreter when the colonel had gone, 'Didn't I tell them a good tale about their goats, hé? In the South they live out in the open and are as well as you or I. But let's talk seriously. Couldn't you get your English to manage an extension of leave for me, to look after their beasts, *hé* ?'

They had begun to build the huts described by the man from the South, when the Indian Corps wrote to Colonel Musgrave that they had discovered a British expert whom they were sending him.

The new seer was an artillery officer, but goats filled his life. Aurelle, who looked after him a good deal, found out that he regarded everything in nature from the point of view of a goat. A Gothic cathedral, according to him, was a poor shelter for goats; not enough air, but that could be remedied by breaking the windows.

His first advice was to mix molasses with the fodder which was given to the animals. It was supposed to fatten them and cure them of that distinguished melancholy which the Indian troops complained of. Large bowls of molasses were therefore distributed to the Hindoo shepherds. The goats remained thin and sad, but the shepherds grew fat. These results surprised the expert.

Then he was shown the plans of the huts. He was astounded.

'If there is one thing in the world that goats cannot do without,' he said, 'it is air. They must have very lofty stables with large windows.'

Colonel Musgrave asked him no more. He thanked him with extreme politeness, then sent for Aurelle.

'Now listen to me,' he said: 'you know Lieutenant Honeysuckle, the goat expert ? Well, I never wish to see him again. I order you to go and find a new farm with him. I forbid you to find it. If you can manage to drown him, to run over him with my car, or to get him eaten by the goats, I will recommend you for the Military

Cross. If he reappears here before my huts are finished, I will have you shot. Be off!'

A week later Lieutenant Honeysuckle broke his leg by falling off his horse in a farmyard. The Territorial from Marseilles was sent back to his corps. As for the goats, one fine day they stopped dying, and no one ever found out why.

CHAPTER XXIV

CRÉCY REVISITED

One morning, Aurelle, seeing an English Staff officer come into his office in a gold-peaked hat with a red band, was surprised and delighted to recognize Major Parker.

'Hullo, sir! I *am* glad to see you again! But you never told me about that'—and he pointed to the signs of authority.

'Well,' said the major, 'I wrote and told you that Colonel Bramble had been made a general. He now commands our old brigade and I am his brigade major. I have just been down to the Base to inspect our reinforcements, and the general ordered me to pick you up on the way back and bring you in to lunch. He will send you back this evening. Your colonel is quite agreeable. We are camped for the moment next to the village where the padre was killed; the general thought you would like to see his grave.'

Two hours later they drew near the front and Aurelle recognized the familiar landmarks: the little English military village with a policeman holding up his hand at every corner; the large market town, scarcely bombarded, but having here and there a roof with its beams exposed; the road, where one occasionally met a man in a flat steel helmet loaded like a mule; the village, the notice boards, 'This road is under observation,' and suddenly, a carefully camouflaged battery barking out of a thicket.

But Major Parker, who had seen these things every day for three years, discoursed on one of his favourite themes:

'The soldier, Aurelle, is always done in by the trades-man and the politician. England will pay ten thousand a year to a lawyer or a banker, but when she has splendid fellows like me who conquer empires and keep them for her, she only gives them just enough to keep their polo ponies. And again——'

'It is just the same in France——' began Aurelle; but the car stopped suddenly opposite the church of a night-mare village, and he recognized H——. 'Poor old village, how it has changed!' he said.

The church, ashamed, now showed its profaned nave; the few houses still standing were merely two triangles of stone sadly facing one another; and the high building of the weaving factory, hit by a shell in the third storey, was bent over like a poplar in a storm.

'Will you follow me?' said the major. 'We have had to put the H.Q. of the brigade outside the village, which was becoming unhealthy. Walk twenty paces behind me; the sausage balloon is up and it's no good showing them the road.'

Aurelle followed for a quarter of an hour through the bushes, and suddenly found himself face to face with General Bramble who, standing at the entrance to a dug-out, was watching a suspicious aeroplane.

'Ah, messiou!' he said. 'That's good!' And the whole of his rugged red face lit up with a kindly smile.

'It will be like lunch in the old days,' he continued, after Aurelle had congratulated him. 'I sent the Staff captain out with the interpreter—for we have another interpreter now, messiou—I thought you would not like

E*

to see him in your place. But he has not really replaced you, messiou; and I telephoned to the Lennox to send the doctor to lunch with us.'

He showed them into the Mess and gave Major Parker a few details of what had been happening.

'Nothing important; they have spoilt the first line a bit at E 17 A. We had a little strafe last night. The division wanted a prisoner, so as to identify the Boche reliefs—yes, yes, that was all right—the Lennox went to fetch him. I have seen the man, but I haven't had their written report yet.'

'What, not since last night?' said Parker. 'What else have they got to do?'

'You see, messiou,' said the general, 'the good old times are over. Parker no longer abuses red hats. No doubt they are abusing him in that little wood you see down there.'

'It is true,' said Parker, 'that one must be on the Staff to realize the importance of work done there. The Staff is really a brain without which no movement of the regiments is possible.'

'You hear, messiou?' said the general. 'It is no longer the same; it will never be the same again. The padre will not be there to talk to us about Scotland and to abuse bishops. And I have no longer got my gramophone, messiou. I left it to the regiment with all my records. The life of the soldier is one of great hardship, messiou, but we had a jolly little Mess with the Lennox, hadn't we?'

The doctor appeared at the entrance to the tent.

'Come in, O'Grady, come in. Late as usual; there is no creature so wicked and so dense as you.'

The lunch was very like those of the good old times—for there were already good old times in this War, which was no longer in the flower of its youth—the orderlies handed boiled potatoes and mutton with mint sauce, and Aurelle had a friendly little discussion with the doctor.

'When do you think war will be finished, Aurelle?' said the doctor.

'When we win,' cut in the general.

But the doctor meant the League of Nations: he did not believe in a final war.

'It is a fairly consistent law of humanity,' he said, 'that men spend about half their lives at war. A Frenchman, called Lapouge, calculated that from the year 1100 to the year 1500, England had been 207 years at war, and 212 years from 1500 to 1900. In France the corresponding figures would be 192 and 181 years.'

'That is very interesting,' said the general.

'According to that same man Lapouge, nineteen million men are killed in war every century. Their blood would fill three million barrels of 180 litres each, and would feed a fountain of blood running 700 litres an hour from the beginning of history.'

'Ugh!' said the general.

'All that does not prove, doctor,' said Aurelle, 'that your fountain will go on running. For many centuries murder has been an institution, and nevertheless courts of justice have been established.'

'Murder,' said the doctor, 'never appears to have been an honoured institution among primitive peoples. Cain had no reason to care for the justice of his country, if I mistake not. Besides, law courts have not suppressed murderers. They punish them, which is not the same thing. A certain number of international conflicts might be settled by civil tribunals, but there will always be wars of passion.'

'Have you read "The Great Illusion"?' said Aurelle.

'Yes,' said the major. 'It's a misleading book. It pretends to show that war is useless, because it is not profitable. We know that very well, but who fights for profit? England did not take part in this war to conquer, but to defend her honour. As for believing that Democracies would be pacific, that's nonsense. A nation worthy of the name is even more susceptible than a monarch. The Royal Era was the age of gold, preceding the Iron Age of the people.'

'There's an argument just like the old days,' said the general. 'Both are right, both are wrong. That's capital! Now, doctor, tell me the story about your going on leave and I shall be perfectly happy.'

After lunch, they all four went to see the padre's grave. It was in a little cemetery surrounded by weeds; the ground broken up here and there by recent shell-holes. The padre lay between two lieutenants of twenty. Cornflowers and other wild plants had spread a living mantle over all three graves.

'After the war,' said General Bramble, 'if I am still alive, I shall have a stone carved with "Here lies a soldier and a sportsman." That will please him.'

The other three remained silent, restraining their emotion with difficulty. Aurelle seemed to hear, in the murmuring summer air, the undying strains of 'Destiny Waltz' and saw the padre setting out once more on horse-back, his pockets bulging with hymn-books and cigarettes for the men. The doctor meditated: ' "Where two or three are gathered together, there I will be in the midst of them." What a profound and true saying! And how the religion of the dead still lives.'

'Come,' said the general, 'we must go, the Boche

[140]

sausage is up in the air, and we are four; it is too many.
They tolerate two, but we must not abuse their courtesy.
I am going on up to the trenches. You, Parker, will take
Aurelle back, and if you want to go with them, doctor,
I will tell your colonel that I have given you leave for
the afternoon.'

The three friends passed slowly across the silent plains,
which only a few months before had been the formidable
battlefield of the Somme. As far as the eye could see,
there were low, undulating hillocks covered with thick,
coarse grass, groups of mutilated tree-trunks marking
the place of the famous wood, and millions of poppies
made these dead fields glow with a warm and coppery
light. A few tenacious rose-trees, with lovely fading roses,
had remained alive in this wilderness, beneath which slept
the dead. Here and there posts, bearing painted notices,
like those on a station platform, recalled villages unknown
yesterday, but now ranking with those of Marathon or
Rivoli: Contalmaison, Martinpuich, Thiepval.

'I hope,' said Aurelle, looking at the innumerable little
crosses, here grouped together as in cemeteries, there
isolated, 'that this ground will be consecrated to the dead
who won it, and that this country will be kept as an
immense rustic cemetery, where children may come to
learn the story of heroes.'

'What an idea!' said the doctor. 'No doubt the graves
will be respected; but they will have good crops all round
them in two years' time. The land is too rich to remain
widowed; look at that superb lot of cornflowers on those
half-healed scars.'

And truly, a little further on, some of the villages
seemed, like convalescents, to be tasting the joy of life
once more. Shop windows crowded with English goods

in many-coloured packets brightened up the ruined houses. As they passed through a straggling village of Spanish aspect the doctor resumed:

'Yes, this is a marvellous land. Every nation in Europe has conquered it in turn; it has defeated its conqueror every time.'

'If we go a little out of the way,' said Parker, 'we could visit the battlefield of Crécy; it would interest me. I hope you are not annoyed with us, Aurelle, for having beaten Philippe de Valois? Your military history is too glorious for you to have any resentment for events which took place so long ago.'

'My oldest resentments do not last six hundred years,' said Aurelle. 'Crécy was an honourably-contested match; we can shake hands over it.'

The chauffeur was told to turn to the west, and they arrived on the site of Crécy by the same lower road taken by Philippe's army.

'The English,' said Parker, 'were drawn up on the hill facing us, their right towards Crécy, their left at Vadicourt, that little village you see down there. They were about thirty thousand; there were a hundred thousand French. The latter appeared about three o'clock in the afternoon, and immediately there was a violent thunderstorm.'

'I observe,' said the doctor, 'that the heavens thought it funny to water an offensive even in those days.'

Parker explained the disposition of the two armies, and the varying fortunes of the battle. Aurelle, who was not listening, admired the woods, the quiet villages, the yellowing grass of the fields, and saw in imagination swarms of men and horses riding up to the assault of this peaceful hill.

'Finally,' concluded the major, 'when the King of France and his army had left the field of battle, Edward invited the principal corps commanders to dinner, and they all ate and drank with great rejoicings because of the good luck which had befallen them.'

'How very English, that invitation to dine at the King's Mess,' said Aurelle.

'Then,' continued Parker, 'he ordered one Renaud de Ghehoben to take all the knights and clerks who knew heraldry——'

'The units,' said the doctor, 'will render to His Majesty's H.Q., not later than this evening a nominal roll of all barons who have passed their hereditary test.'

'And commanded them to count the dead, and to write down the names of all the knights whom they could recognize.'

'The adjutant-general will compile a return of noble persons who have been killed, stating their rank,' said the doctor.

'Renaud found eleven princes, thirteen hundred knights and sixteen thousand foot soldiers.'

Heavy black clouds were showing up against the brilliant sunshine: a storm was coming over the hill. By the valley of Renaud's clerks, they climbed up on to the summit and Parker looked for the tower from which Edward had watched the battle.

'I thought,' he said, 'that it had been made into a mill, but I don't see one on the horizon.'

Aurelle, noticing a few old peasants, helped by children, cutting corn in the next field, went up to them and asked them where the tower was.

'The tower? There is no tower in these parts,' one of them said, 'nor mill either.'

'Perhaps we are wrong,' said the major. 'Ask him if this is really where the battle was.'

'The battle?' replied the old man. 'What battle?'

And the people of Crécy turned back to their work, binding into neat sheaves the corn of this invincible land.

THE VERSE IN THE ORIGINAL

Page 26

'La Mort passe; le Destin chante;
    Vite, oublie-moi.
Tes robes noires sont charmantes;
    Mets-les six mois.

Garde-toi de venir en pleurs
    M'offrir des roses;
Aux vivants réserve tes fleurs
    Et toutes choses.

Ne me plains pas, je dormirai
    Sans barcaroles,
Et de mon corps je nourrirai
    Des herbes folles. . . .

Mais si, par quelque soir d'automne
    Ou de brouillard,
Pour ton visage de madone
    Tu veux le fard

De cet air de mélancolie
    Que j'aimais tant,
Alors oublie que tu m'oublies
    Pour un instant.'

Les soldats passent en chantant:
'Mets tes soucis dans ta musette.'*
Il pleut, il vente, il fait un temps
A ne pas suivre une grisette.
Les soldats passent en chantant,
Moi, je fais des vers pour Josette;
Les soldats passent en chantant:
'Mets tes soucis dans ta musette.'

Un planton va dans un instant
M'apporter de vieilles gazettes:
Vieux discours de vieux charlatans,
'Mets tes soucis dans ta musette.'
Nous passons nos plus beaux printemps
A ces royales amusettes;
Les soldats passent en chantant;
'Mets tes soucis dans ta musette.'

La pluie, sur les vitres battant
Orchestre, comme une mazette,
Quelque prélude de Tristan,
'Mets tes soucis dans ta musette.'
Demain sans doute un percutant
M'enverra faire la causette
Aux petits soupers de Satan.
'Mets tes soucis dans ta musette.'
Les soldats passent en chantant.

* 'Pack up your troubles in your old kit-bag.'

*Dans votre salon directoire
(Bleu lavande et jaune citron)
De vieux fauteuils voisineront
Dans un style contradictoire
Avec un divan sans histoire
(Bleu lavende et jaune citron).*

*A des merveilleuses notoires
(Bleu lavande et jaune citron)
Des muscadins à cinq chevrons
Diront la prochaine victoire,
En des domains ostentatoires
(Bleu lavande et jaune citron).*

*Les murs nus comme un mur d'église
(Bleu lavande et jaune citron)
Quelque temps encore attendront
Qu'un premier consul brutalise
Leur calme et notre Directoire
De son visage péremptoire
(Œil bleu lavande et teint citron).*

Puisque le mauvais temps vous condamne à la chambre,
Puisque vous méprisez désormais les romans,
Puisque pour mon bonheur vous n'avez pas d'amant,
Et puisque ce mois d'août s'obstine impunément
A jouer les décembre.

Je griffonne pour vous ces vers sans queue ni tête,
Sans rime, ou peu s'en faut, en tout cas sans raison,
Que j'intitulerai dans mes œuvres complètes:
'Discours pour une amie qui garde la maison
Par un jour de tempête.'

Je ne sais là-dessus si nous sentons de même,
Mais quand je suis ainsi rêveur et paresseux,
Quand il pleut dans mon cœur comme il pleut dans——

Page 83

O mûre et charmante épicière
    Au corsage gonflé
Et vous, jolie garde-barrière,
    Aux bras nus et musclés,

Institutrice aux yeux mi-clos,
    Aux robes citadines,
Vous qui possédiez un piano
    Et de longues mains fines,

Boulangère à qui les écus
    Ne coûtaient certes guère,
Car vous vous mettiez au-dessus
    Des préjugés vulgaires,

Ah ! que vos charmes villageois
    Nous furent donc utiles
Pour vaincre le cafard sournois
    De ces journées hostiles !

Accoudés à votre comptoir
    Et parlant pour nous-mêmes,
Nous vous disions nos longs espoirs
    Et nos vastes problèmes.

Vous n'avez pas souvent compris,
    Mais soyez bien tranquilles,
Nos belles amies de Paris
    Ne sont pas plus habiles.

L'homme croit toujours émouvoir
La femme qu'il désire:
Elle n'est pour lui qu'un miroir
Dans lequel il s'admire,

Et quand Margot, l'air résigné,
Subit nos hypothèses,
Elle vaut bien la Sévigné,
Pourvu qu'elle se taise.

Page 89

Demain, départ de la brigade
La cornemuse et le tambour
Donneront la dernière aubade
A ces fugitives amours.
Les montagnards aux beaux genoux,
Qui mimaient la danse du sable
Avec des chants graves et doux
Vont danser la ronde du Diable.

La Victoire, un jour, les cherchant,
Les trouvera trois pieds sous terre,
Mais par ces fermes et ces champs
Flottera leur ombre légère.

Et dans nos villages des Flandres . . .

CHANSON DU COMTE DE DORSET
(1665)

En cet instant, belles personnes,
Un adolescent bien poudré
A coup sûr près de vous fredonne
La chanson que vous adorez.
        Fa, do, sol, ré.

En caressant ses cheveux lisses
Avec des gestes maniérés,
Il vous fait des yeux en coulisse
Et des regards énamourés
        Fa, do, sol, ré.

La vague cependant balance
Notre vieux bateau délabré,
Le vent qui siffle avec violence
Chante notre Miserere.
        Fa, do, sol, ré.

En vain, pour conjurer l'image
D'un sort, hélas ! trop assuré,
Accrochés à nos bastingages,
Nous fredonnons désespérés.
        Fa, do, sol, ré.

Poussés vers les sombres royaumes
Par votre oubli prématuré,
Le plus lamentable des psaumes
Chante en notre cœur ulcéré:
        Fa, do, sol, ré.

Quoi ? Votre âme était si petite
Et votre amour si mesuré ?
Vous avez oublié si vite
Que ce fut notre air préféré,
      Fa, do, sol, ré.

En semblable cas, les Romaines
Restaient prés du foyer sacré
Et chantaient en filant la laine
Des hymnes aux dieux ignorés.
      Fa, do, sol, ré.

Ne pouvez-vous faire comme elles ?
Oh ! dites que vous le voudrez
Et qu'en des amours éternelles
Pour nous seuls vous vous garderez.
      Fa, do, sol, ré.

Car si vous êtes inconstantes
Comme ces flots désemparés,
Craignez qu'un jour le doux andante
Ne devienne un Dies iræ.
      Fa, do, sol, ré.

Tu l'as dit, ô Pascal, le nez de Cléopâtre,
S'il eût été plus court . . . nous n'en serions pas là.

Croyez pas que je moralise,
Si je vous envoie ces bobards,
C'est que notre Mess analyse
Ce soir la question du hasard . . .

Page 121

Pourquoi me fermes-tu les yeux
Lorsque tu me baises la bouche ?

Page 129

Le jardin provincial s'endort dans le soir tendre;
Un violon d'enfant joue 'J'ai du bon tabac';
Les cloches lentement tintent; l'on peut entendre
Vibrer dans l'air lointain le bruit sourd des combats.

Une étoile s'allume en un ciel qui grisaille;
Un arbre aux fins rameaux sur l'occident dessine
Un croquis japonais que la lune termine;
Une voix chante; un chien aboie; l'ombre tressaille.

La vie semble si douce en ce calme vallon
Que si l'homme n'avait, hélas! trop de mémoire,
Par un tel soir paisible il pourrait presque croire
Que ce monde menteur est l'œuvre d'un Dieu bon.

Cependant, par delà ces collines flexibles
Et sous ce même ciel au calme décevant,
A quelques lieues d'ici, par ce beau soir paisible
Les portes de l'enfer s'ouvrent pour des vivants.

THE DISCOURSES OF
DOCTOR O'GRADY

*Translated from the French
by Jules Castier and
Ronald Boswell*

CONTENTS

    I Portraits, 161

   II Diplomacy, 169

  III The Tower of Babel, 174

  IV A Business Man in the Army, 179

   V The Story of Private Biggs, 186

  VI An Air Raid, 191

 VII Love and the Infant Dundas, 196

VIII A Great Chef, 202

  IX Prélude a la Soirée d'un Général, 207

   X Private Brommit's Conversion, 212

  XI Justice, 219

 XII Variations, 224

XIII The Cure, 229

 XIV The Beginning of the End, 236

  XV Danse Macabre, 243

 XVI The Glory of the Garden, 248

XVII Letter from Colonel Parker to Aurelle, 255

XVIII General Bramble's Return, 259

CHAPTER I

PORTRAITS

'As to what the picture represents,
that depends upon who looks at it.'
WHISTLER

The French Mission in its profound wisdom had sent as liaison officer to the Scottish Division a captain of Dragoons whose name was Beltara.

'Are you any relation to the painter, sir?' Aurelle, the interpreter, asked him.

'What did you say?' said the dragoon. 'Say that again, will you? You *are* in the army, aren't you? You are a soldier, for a little time at any rate? and you claim to know that such people as painters exist? You actually admit the existence of that God-forsaken species?'

And he related how he had visited the French War Office after he had been wounded, and how an old colonel had made friends with him and had tried to find him a congenial job.

'What's your profession in civilian life, *capitaine*?' the old man had asked as he filled in a form.

'I am a painter, sir.'

'A painter?' the colonel exclaimed, dumbfounded. 'A painter? Why, damn it all!'

And after thinking it over for a minute he added, with the kindly wink of an accomplice in crime, 'Well, let's put down *nil*, eh? It won't look quite so silly.'

F

Captain Beltara and Aurelle soon became inseparable companions. They had the same tastes and different professions, which is the ideal recipe for friendship. Aurelle admired the sketches in which the painter recorded the flexible lines of the Flemish landscape; Beltara was a kindly critic of the young man's rather feeble verses.

'You would perhaps be a poet,' he said to him, 'if you were not burdened with a certain degree of culture. An artist must be an idiot. The only perfect ones are the sculptors; then come the landscape painters; then painters in general; after them the writers. The critics are not at all stupid; and the really intelligent men never do anything.'

'Why shouldn't intelligence have an art of its own, as sensibility has?'

'No, my friend, no. Art is a game; intelligence is a profession. Look at me, for instance; now that I no longer touch my brushes, I sometimes actually catch myself thinking; it's quite alarming.'

'You ought to paint some portraits here, *mon capitaine*. Aren't you tempted? These sunburnt British complexions——'

'Of course, my boy, it is tempting; but I haven't got my things with me. Besides, would they consent to sit?'

'Of course they would, for as long as you like. To-morrow I'll bring round young Dundas, the aide-de-camp. He's got nothing to do; he'll be delighted.'

Next day Beltara made a three-crayon sketch of Lieutenant Dundas. The young aide-de-camp turned out quite a good sitter; all he asked was to be allowed to do something, which meant shouting his hunting cries, cracking his favourite whip and talking to his dog.

'Ah,' said Aurelle, at the end of the sitting, 'I like that immensely—really. It's so lightly touched—it's a mere nothing, and yet the whole of England is there.'

And, waving his hands with the ritual gestures of the infatuated picture-lover, he praised the artlessness of the clear, wide eyes, the delightful freshness of the complexion, and the charming candour of the smile.

But the Cherub planted himself in front of his portrait, struck the classical pose of the golfer, and, poising his arms and hitting at an imaginary ball, pronounced judgment on the work of art with perfect frankness.

'My God,' he said, 'what an awful thing! How the deuce did you see, old man, that my breeches were laced at the side?'

'What on earth can that matter?' asked Aurelle, annoyed.

'Matter! Would *you* like to be painted with your nose behind your ear? My God! It's about as much like me as it is like Lloyd George.'

'Likeness is quite a secondary quality,' said Aurelle condescendingly. 'The interesting thing is not the individual; it is the type, the synthesis of a whole race or class.'

'In the days when I was starving in my native South,' said the painter, 'I used to paint portraits of tradesmen's wives for a fiver. When I had done, the family assembled for a private view. "Well," said the husband, "it's not so bad; but what about the likeness, eh? You put it in afterwards, I suppose?" "The likeness?" I indigantly replied. "The likeness? My dear sir, I am a painter of ideals; I don't paint your wife as she is, I paint her as she ought to be. Your wife? Why, you see her every day—she cannot interest you. But my painting—ah, you never saw anything like my painting!" And the tradesman was convinced, and went about repeating in every café on the Cannebière, "Beltara, *mon bon*, is the painter of ideals; he does not paint my wife as she is, he paints her as she ought to be."'

'Well,' interrupted young Lieutenant Dundas, 'if you can make my breeches lace in front, I should be most grateful. I look like a damned fool as it is now!'

The following week Beltara, who had managed to get hold of some paints, made excellent studies in oil of Colonel Parker and Major Knight. The major, who was stout, found his corporation somewhat exaggerated.

'Yes,' said the painter, 'but with the varnish, you know——'

And with an expressive movement of his hands he made as if to restore the figure to more normal dimensions.

The colonel, who was lean, wanted to be padded out.

'Yes,' said Beltara, 'but with the varnish, you know——'

And his hands, moving back again, gave promise of astonishing expansions.

Having regained a taste for his profession, he tried his hand at some of the finest types in the Division. His portraits met with various verdicts; each model thought his own rotten and the others excellent.

The Divisional Squadron Commander found his boots badly polished. The C.R.E. commented severely on the important mistakes in the order of his ribbons; the Legion of Honour being a foreign order should not have preceded the Bath, and the Japanese Rising Sun ought to have followed the Italian Order for Valour.

The only unqualified praise came from the sergeant-major who acted as chief clerk to General Bramble. He was a much-beribboned old warrior with a head like a faun and three red hairs on top of it. He had the respectful familiarity of the underling who knows he is indispensable, and he used to come in at all times of the day and criticize the captain's work.

'That's fine, sir,' he would say, 'that's fine.'

After some time he asked Aurelle whether the captain would consent 'to take his photo.' The request was accepted, for the old N.C.O.'s beacon-like countenance tempted the painter, and he made a kindly caricature.

'Well, sir,' the old soldier said to him, 'I've seen lots of photographer chaps the likes of you—I've seen lots at fairs in Scotland—but I've never seen one as gives you a portrait so quick.'

He soon told General Bramble of the painter's prowess; and as he exercised a respectful but all-powerful authority over the general, he persuaded him to come and give the French liaison officer a sitting.

The general proved an admirable model of discipline. Beltara, who was very anxious to be successful in this attempt, demanded several sittings. The general arrived punctually, took up his pose with charming deliberation, and when the painter had done, said 'Thank you,' with a smile, and went away without saying another word.

'Look here,' Beltara said to Aurelle, 'does this bore him or not? He hasn't come one single time to look at what I have done. I can't understand it.'

'He'll look at it when you've finished,' Aurelle replied. 'I'm sure he's delighted, and he'll let you see it when the time comes.'

As a matter of fact after the last sitting, when the painter had said 'Thank you, sir, I think I could only spoil it now,' the general slowly descended from the platform, took a few solemn steps round the easel, and stared at his portrait for some minutes.

'Humph!' he said at length, and left the room.

Dr O'Grady, who was a man of real artistic culture, seemed somehow to understand that keeping decorations in their correct order is not the only criterion of the beauty of a portrait. The grateful Beltara proposed to make a sketch of him, and during the sitting was pleased to find himself in agreement with the doctor upon many things.

'The main point,' said the painter, 'is to see simply—outlines, general masses. The thing is not to copy nature with childish minuteness.'

'No, of course not,' replied the doctor. 'Besides, it can't be done.'

'Of course it can't, because nature is so endlessly full of details which can never all be considered. The thing is to suggest their presence.'

'Quite so,' said the doctor.

But when he came to gaze upon the face he loved so well, and saw it transformed into outlines and general masses, he seemed a little surprised.

'Well, of course,' he said, 'it is excellent—oh, it's very, very good—but don't you think you have made me a little too old? I have no lines at the corner of my mouth, and my hair is not quite so thin.'

He appealed to the aide-de-camp who was just then passing by.

'Dundas, is this like me?'

'Certainly, Doc; but it's ten years younger.'

The doctor's smile darkened, and he began rather insistently to praise the Old Masters.

'Modern painting,' he proclaimed, 'is too brutal.'

'Good heavens,' said Aurelle, 'a great artist cannot paint with a powder-puff; you must be able to feel that the fellow with the pencil was not a eunuch.'

'Really,' he went on, when the doctor had left in rather a bad temper, 'he's as ridiculous as the others. I think his portrait is very vigorous, and not in the least a skit, whatever he may say.'

'Just sit down there a minute, old man,' said the painter. 'I shall be jolly glad to work from an intelligent model for once. They all want to look like tailors' fashion-plates. Now, I can't change my style; I don't paint in beauty paste, I render what I see—it's like Diderot's old story about the amateur who asked a floral painter to portray a lion. "With pleasure," said the artist, "but you may expect a lion that will be as like a rose as I can make him."'

The conversation lasted a long time; it was friendly and technical. Aurelle praised Beltara's painting; Beltara expressed his joy at having found so penetrating and artistic a critic in the midst of so many Philistines.

'I prefer your opinion to a painter's; it's certainly more sincere. Would you mind turning your profile a bit more towards me? Some months before the war I had two friends in my studio to whom I wished to show a little picture I intended for the *Salon*. "Yes," said the younger of them, "it's all right, but there ought to be a light spot in that corner; your lights are not well balanced." "Shut up, you fool," the other whispered to him, "that'll make it *really* good!" Come on, old man, come and look; I think that sketch can be left as it is.'

Aurelle walked up to the painter, and, cocking his head on one side, looked at the drawing.

'It's charming,' he said at last with some reluctance. 'It's charming. There are some delightful touches—all that still life on the table, it might be a Chardin—and I like the background very much indeed.'

'Well, old man, I'm glad you like it. Take it back with you when you go on leave and give it to your wife.'

'Er——' sighed Aurelle, 'thank you, *mon capitaine*; it's really very kind of you. Only—you'll think me no end of a fool—you see, if it is to be for my wife, I'd like you to touch up the profile just a little. Of course you understand.'

And Beltara, who was a decent fellow, adorned his friend's face with the Grecian nose and the small mouth which the gods had denied him.

CHAPTER II

DIPLOMACY

'We are not foreigners; we are English;
it is *you* that are foreigners,
AN ENGLISH LADY ABROAD

When Dr O'Grady and Aurelle had succeeded, with some difficulty, in obtaining a room from old Madame de Vauclère, Colonel Parker went over to see them and was charmed with the château and the park.

France and England, he said, were the only two countries in which fine gardens were to be found, and he told the story of the American who asked the secret of those well-mown lawns and was answered, 'Nothing is simpler: water them for twelve hundred years.'

Then he inquired timidly whether he also might not be quartered at the château.

'It wouldn't do very well, sir; Madame is mortally afraid of new-comers, and she has a right, being a widow, to refuse to billet you.'

'Aurelle, my boy, do be a good fellow, and go and arrange matters.'

After much complaining, Madame de Vauclère consented to put the colonel up: all her sons were officers, and she could not withstand sentimental arguments for very long.

The next day Parker's orderly joined the doctor's in the château kitchen, and together they annexed the fire-

F*

place. To make room for their own utensils, they took down a lot of comical little French articles, removed what they saw no use for, put the kettle on, and whistled hymns as they filled the cupboards with tins of boot polish in scientifically graded rows.

After adoring them on the first day, putting up with them on the second, and cursing them on the third, the old cook came up to Aurelle with many lamentations, and dwelt at some length on the sad state of her saucepans; but she found the interpreter dealing with far more serious problems.

Colonel Parker, suddenly realizing that it was inconvenient for the general to be quartered away from his Staff, had decided to transfer the whole H.Q. to the château of Vauclère.

'Explain to the old lady that I want a very good room for the general, and the billiard-room for our clerks.'

'Why, it's impossible, sir; she has no good rooms left.'

'What about her own?' said Colonel Parker.

Madame de Vauclère, heart-broken, but vanquished by the magic word 'General,' which Aurelle kept on repeating sixty times a minute, tearfully abandoned her canopied bed and her red damask chairs, and took refuge on the second floor.

Meanwhile the drawing-room with its ancient tapestries was filled with an army of phlegmatic clerks occupied in heaping up innumerable cases containing the history in triplicate of the Division, its men, horses, arms and achievements.

'Maps' set up his drawing-board on a couple of armchairs; 'Intelligence' concealed their secrets in an Aubusson boudoir; and the telephone men sauntered about in the dignified, slow, bantering fashion of the

British workman. They set up their wires in the park, and cut branches off the oaks and lime trees; they bored holes in the old walls, and, as they wished to sleep near their work, they put up tents on the lawns.

The Staff asked for their horses; and the animals were picketed in the garden walks, as the stables were too small. In the garden the Engineers made a dug-out in case of a possible bombardment. The orderlies' football developed a distinct liking for the window-panes of the summer house. The park assumed the aspect first of a building site and then of a training camp, and new-comers said, 'These French gardens *are* badly kept!'

This methodical work of destruction had been going on for about a week when 'Intelligence' got going.

'Intelligence' was represented at the Division by Captain Forbes.

Forbes, who had never yet arrested a real spy, saw potential spies everywhere, and as he was fond of the company of the great, he always made his suspicions a pretext for going to see General Bramble or Colonel Parker. One day he remained closeted for an hour with the colonel, who summoned Aurelle as soon as he had left.

'Do you know,' he said to him, 'there are most dangerous things going on here. Two old women are constantly being seen in this château. What the deuce are they up to?'

'What do you mean?' gasped Aurelle. 'This is their house, sir; it's Madame de Vauclère and her maid.'

'Well, you go and tell them from me to clear out as soon as possible. The presence of civilians among a Staff cannot be tolerated; the Intelligence people have complained about it, and they are perfectly right.'

'But where are they to go to, sir?'

'That's no concern of mine.'

Aurelle turned round furiously and left the room. Coming across Dr O'Grady in the park, he asked his advice about the matter.

'Why, doctor, she had a perfect right to refuse to billet us, and from a military point of view we should certainly be better off at Nieppe. She was asked to do us a favour, she grants it, and her kindness is taken as a reason for her expulsion! I can't "evacuate her to the rear," as Forbes would say; she'd die of it!'

'I should have thought,' said the doctor, 'that after three years you knew the British temperament better than this. Just go and tell the colonel, politely and firmly, that you refuse to carry out his orders. Then depict Madame de Vauclère's situation in your grandest and most tragic manner. Tell him her family has been living in the château for the last two thousand years, that one of her ancestors came over to England with William the Conqueror, and that her grandfather was a friend of Queen Victoria's. Then the colonel will apologize and place a whole wing at the disposal of your *protégée*.'

Dr O'Grady's prescription was carried out in detail by Aurelle with most satisfactory results.

'You are right,' said the colonel, 'Forbes is a damned idiot. The old lady can stay on, and if anybody annoys her, let her come to me.'

'It's all these servants who are such a nuisance to her, sir,' said Aurelle. 'It's very painful for her to see her own house turned upside-down.'

'Upside-down?' gasped the colonel. 'Why, the house is far better kept than it was in her time. I have had the water in the cisterns analysed; I have had sweet-peas planted and the tennis lawn rolled. What can she complain of?'

In the well-appointed kitchen garden, where stout-limbed pear trees bordered square beds of sprouting lettuce, Aurelle joined O'Grady.

'Doctor, you're a great man, and my old lady is saved. But it appears she ought to thank her lucky stars for having placed her under the British Protectorate, which, in exchange for her freedom, provides her with a faultless tennis lawn and microbeless water.'

'There is nothing,' said the doctor gravely, 'that the British Government is not ready to do for the good of the natives.'

CHAPTER III

THE TOWER OF BABEL

'Des barques romaines, disais-je.—Non, disais-tu, portugaises.'
JEAN GIRAUDOUX

'Wot you require, sir,' interrupted Private Brommit, 'is a glass o' boilin' 'ot milk an' whisky, with lots o' cinnamon.'

Aurelle, who was suffering from an attack of influenza, was at Estrées, under the care of Dr O'Grady, who tirelessly prescribed ammoniated quinine.

'I say, doctor,' said the young Frenchman, 'this is a drug that's utterly unknown in France. It seems strange that medicines should have a nationality.'

'Why shouldn't they?' said the doctor. 'Many diseases are national. If a Frenchman has a bathe after a meal, he is stricken with congestion of the stomach and is drowned. An Englishman never has congestion of the stomach.'

'No,' said Aurelle; 'he is drowned all the same, but his friends say he had cramp, and the honour of Britain is saved.'

Private Brommit knocked at the door and showed in Colonel Parker, who sat down by the bed and asked Aurelle how he was getting on.

'He is much better,' said the doctor; 'a few more doses of quinine——'

'I am glad to hear that,' replied the colonel, 'because

[174]

I shall want you, Aurelle. G.H.Q. is sending me on a mission for a fortnight to one of your Brittany ports; I am to organize the training of the Portuguese Division. I have orders to take an interpreter with me. I thought of you for the job.'

'But,' Aurelle put in, 'I don't know a word of Portuguese.'

'What does that matter?' said the colonel. 'You're an interpreter, aren't you? Isn't that enough?'

The following day Aurelle told his servant to try and find a Portuguese in the little town of Estrées.

'Brommit is an admirable fellow,' said Colonel Parker, 'he found whisky for me in the middle of the bush, and quite drinkable beer in France. If I say to him, "Don't come back without a Portuguese," he is sure to bring one with him, dead or alive.'

As a matter of fact, that very evening he brought back with him a nervous, talkative little man.

'Ze Poortooguez in fifteen days,' exclaimed the little man, gesticulating freely with his small plump hands. 'A language so rich, so flexible, in fifteen days! Ah, you have ze luck, young man, to 'ave found in zis town Juan Garretos, of Portalègre, Master of Arts of ze University of Coimbra, and positivist philosopher. Ze Poortooguez in fifteen days! Do you know at least ze Low Latin? ze Greek? ze Hebrew? ze Arabic? ze Chinese? If not, it is useless to go furzer.'

Aurelle confessed his ignorance.

'Never mind,' said Juan Garretos indulgently; 'ze shape of your 'ead inspire me wiz confidence: for ten francs ze hour I accept you. Only, mind, no chattering; ze Latins talk too much. Not a single word of ze English between us now. *Faz favor d'fallar Portuguez*—do me ze favour of speaking ze Poortooguez. Know first zat, in ze Poortooguez, one speak in ze zird person. You must call your speaker "Excellency".'

'What's that?' Aurelle interrupted. 'I thought you had just had a democratic revolution.'

'Precisely,' said the positivist philosopher, wringing his little hands, 'precisely. In France you made ze revoluçaoung in order zat every man should be called "citizen". What a waste of energy! In Poortugal we made ze revoluçaoung in order zat every man should be called "His Highness". Instead of levelling down we levelled up. It is better. Under ze old order ze children of ze poor were *rapachos*, and zose of ze aristocracy were *meninos*: now zey are all *meninos*. Zat is a revoluçaoung! *Faz favor d'fallar Portuguez*. Ze Latins always talk too much.'

Having thus earned his ten francs by an hour's unceasing eloquence, he made a fairer proposal to Aurelle next day.

'I will arrange with you for a fixed sum,' he said. 'If I teach you two souzand words, you give me fifty francs.'

'Very well,' replied Aurelle, 'two thousand words will be a sufficient vocabulary to begin with.'

'All right,' said Juan Garretos; 'now listen to me. All ze words which in ze English end with "tion" are ze same in ze Poortooguez wiz ze ending "çaoung." Revolution — *revoluçaoung*; constitution — *constituçaoung* inquisition—*inquisiçaoung*. Now zere are in ze English two souzand words ending in "tion." Your Excellency owes me fifty francs. *Faz favor d'fallar Portuguez*.'

A fortnight later Colonel Parker and Aurelle stepped

on to the platform at B——, where they were met by Major Baraquin, the officer commanding the garrison, and Captain Pereira, the Portuguese liaison officer.

Major Baraquin was a very old soldier. He had seen service—in the 1870 campaign. All strangers, Allies included, inspired him with a distrust which even his respect for his superiors failed to remove. When the French War Office ordered him to place his barracks at the disposal of a British colonel, discipline required him to obey, but hostile memories inspired him with savage resistance.

'After all, sir,' said Aurelle to Parker, 'his grandfather was at Waterloo.'

'Are you quite sure,' asked the colonel, 'that he was not there himself?'

Above all things, Major Baraquin would never admit that the armies of other nations might have different habits from his own. That the British soldier should eat jam and drink tea filled him with generous indignation.

'The colonel,' Aurelle translated, 'requests me to ask you . . .'

'No, no, *no*,' replied Major Baraquin in stentorian tones, without troubling to listen any further.

'But it will be necessary, sir, for the Portuguese who are going to land. . . .'

'No, no, *no*, I tell you,' Major Baraquin repeated, resolved upon ignoring demands which he considered subversive and childish. This refrain was as far as he ever got in his conversations with Aurelle.

Next day several large British transports arrived, and disgorged upon the quay thousands of small, black-haired men who gazed mournfully upon the alien soil.

It was snowing, and most of them were seeing snow for the first time in their lives. They wandered about in the mud, shivering in their spotted blue cotton uniforms and dreaming, no doubt, of sunny Alemtejo.

'They'll fight well,' said Captain Pereira, 'they'll fight well. Wellington called them his fighting cocks, and Napoleon said his Portuguese legion made the best troops in the world. But can you wonder they are sad?'

Each of them had brought with him a pink handkerchief containing his collection of souvenirs—little reminders of his village, his people, or his best girl—and when they were told that they could not take their pink parcels with them to the front, there was a heart-breaking outcry.

Major Baraquin, with unconscious and sinister humour, had quartered them in the shambles.

'It would be better——' began Colonel Parker.

'Il vaudrait peut-être mieux——' Aurelle attempted to translate.

'Vossa Excellencia——' began Captain Pereira.

'No, no, *no*,' said the old warrior passionately.

The Portuguese went to the shambles.

CHAPTER IV

A BUSINESS MAN IN THE ARMY

'The reasonable man adapts himself to the world; the unreasonable one persists in trying to adapt the world to himself. Therefore all progress depends on the unreasonable man.'

G. B. SHAW (*A Revolutionist's Handbook*)

Colonel Musgrave of the R.A.S.C. had been instructed to superintend the supply and transport arrangements of the Portuguese Division, and Lieutenant Barefoot, in charge of a Labour Company, had been detailed to assist him.

'These men,' he explained to Colonel Musgrave, 'are all Southampton dockers. In peace time I am their employer, and Sergeant Scott over there is their foreman. They tell me your Labour Companies have often shown rather poor discipline. There's no fear of anything like that with my men; they have been chosen with care, and look up to me as if I were a king. Scott, my sergeant, can do anything; neither he nor my men ever drink a drop. As for me, I am a real business man, and I intend to introduce new methods into the army.'

Barefoot was fifty years old; he had a bald head shaped like an egg. He had just enlisted to serve his King and country, and was overflowing with goodwill.

The next morning twenty of his men were dead-drunk, two were absent at roll-call, and Sergeant Scott had a scar on his nose which seemed to be the result of a somewhat sudden encounter with mother earth.

'No matter,' said the worthy N.C.O., 'Barefoot is an ass, and never notices anything.'

Next day the first batch of Portuguese troops arrived. British tugs towed the huge transports round the tiny harbour with graceful ease, and the decks seethed with masses of troops. The harbour captain and the *Ponts et Chaussées* engineer were loud in protest against these wonders, as being 'contrary to the ideas of the Service.' The wharves were filled with motor lorries, mountains of pressed hay, sacks of oats and boxes of biscuits.

Colonel Musgrave, who was to take charge of this treasure-store, began to make his plan of campaign.

'Tomorrow, Friday,' he said, 'there will be a parade on the wharf at 7 a.m. I shall hold an inspection myself before work is begun.'

On Friday morning at seven, Barefoot, his labourers and the lorries were all paraded on the wharf in excellent order. At eight the colonel got up, had his bath and shaved. Then he partook of eggs and bacon, bread and jam, and drank two cups of tea. Towards nine o'clock his car took him to the wharf. When he saw the men standing motionless, the officer saluting and the lorries all in a row, his face went as red as a brick, and he stood up in his car and addressed them angrily:

'So you are incapable of the slightest initiative! If I am absent for an hour, detained by more important work, everything comes to a standstill! I see I cannot rely on anyone here except myself!'

The same evening he called the officers together.

'Tomorrow, Saturday,' he said, 'there will be a parade at 7 a.m.—and this time I shall be there.'

The next morning Barefoot with his men and lorries paraded once more on the wharf, with a sea-wind sweeping an icy rain into their faces. At half-past seven the lieutenant took action.

'We will start work,' he said. 'The colonel was quite right yesterday and spoke like a real business man. In our respect for narrow formalism, we stupidly wasted a whole morning's work.'

So his men began to pile up the cases, the lorries started to move the sacks of oats, and the day's work was pretty well advanced when Colonel Musgrave appeared. Having had his bath and shaved, and absorbed poached eggs on toast, bread, marmalade and three cups of tea, he had not been able to be ready before ten. Suddenly coming upon all this healthy bustle, he leaped out of his car, and angrily addressed the eager Barefoot, who was approaching him with a modest smile.

'Who has had the impudence to call the men off parade before my arrival?' he said. 'So if I happen to be detained elsewhere by more important work, my orders are simply disregarded! I see again that I cannot rely on anyone here except myself!'

Meanwhile the crestfallen Barefoot was meditating upon the mysterious ways of the army. Musgrave inspected the work and decided that everything was to be done all over again. The biscuits were to be put in the shed where the oats had been piled, and the oats were to be put out in the open where the biscuits had been. The meat was to change places with the jam, and the mustard with the bacon. The lorries were to take away again everything they had just brought up. So that when lunchtime arrived, everything was in exactly the same state as it had been at dawn. The Admiralty announced the arrival of a transport at two o'clock; the men were supposed to find their rations ready for them upon landing.

Musgrave very pluckily decided that the Labour Company were to have no rest, and were just to be content with nibbling a light lunch while they went on with their work.

Barefoot, who had got up at six and was very hungry, approached the colonel in fear and trembling.

'May I leave my sergeant in charge for half an hour, sir?' he asked. 'He can do everything as well as I can. I should like just to run along to the nearest café and have something to eat.'

Musgrave gazed at him in mournful astonishment.

'Really,' he said, 'you young fellows don't seem to realize that there's a war on.' Whereupon he stepped into his car and drove off to the hotel.

Barefoot, somewhat downcast, buttonholed the interpreter, who was father-confessor to all Englishmen in distress. Aurelle begged him not to get excited.

'You are always talking about introducing your business methods into the army. As if that were possible! Why, the objects of the two things are entirely different. A business man is always looking for work; an officer is always trying to avoid it. If you neglect these principles, I can foresee an ignominious end in store for you, Barefoot, and Colonel Musgrave will trample on your corpse.'

Now the thirty thousand Portuguese had been fed during their long voyage on tinned food; and as the transports' holds were being cleared, innumerable empty tins began to accumulate on the wharves. Barefoot and his men were ordered to gather these tins together into regular heaps. These grew so rapidly that the Mayor of the town was exceedingly concerned to see such a waste of space in a harbour already filled to bursting-point, and sent a pointed letter to Colonel Musgrave, asking him to find some other place for his empty tins.

Colonel Musgrave ordered his interpreter to write an equally pointed letter, reminding the Mayor of B—— that the removal of refuse was a municipal concern, and that the British Army was therefore waiting for the Town to hand over a plot of ground for the purpose.

Barefoot happened to speak of this difficulty one day to the business man at whose house he was billeted; and the latter told him that a process had recently been discovered by which old tins could be melted down and used again, and that a company had been floated to work out the scheme; they would be sure to purchase Colonel Musgrave's tins.

The enthusiastic Barefoot began to see visions of profitable and glorious enterprises. Not only would he rid his chief and the Mayor of B—— of a lot of cumbersome salvage, but this modest contract for some tens of tons might well serve as a model to those responsible for the sale of the millions of empty tins scattered daily by the British Army over the plains of Flanders and Artois. And the Commander-in-Chief would call the attention of the War Office to the fact that 'Lieutenant E. W. Barefoot, by his bold and intelligent initiative, had enabled salvage to be carried out to the extent of several million pounds.'

'Aurelle,' he said to the interpreter, 'let's write to this company immediately; we'll speak about it to the colonel when we get their reply.'

The answer came by return; they were offered twenty francs per ton, carriage at the company's cost.

Barefoot explained his scheme to Colonel Musgrave with assumed modesty, adding that it would be a good thing to flatten out the tins before dispatching them, and that Sergeant Scott, who was a handy man, could easily undertake the job.

'First of all,' said the colonel, 'why can't you mind your own business? Don't you know you are forbidden to correspond with strangers upon matters pertaining to the service without consulting your superior officers? And who told you *I*'ve not been thinking for quite a long time of selling your damned tins? Do you think things are as simple as all that in the Army? Fetch Aurelle; I'm going to see the superintendent of the French Customs.'

Three years' experience had taught Colonel Musgrave that the French Customs Service were always to be relied on.

'Kindly ask this gentleman whether the British Army, having imported tins with their contents without paying any duty, has the right to sell these tins empty in France?'

'No,' answered the official, when the colonel's question had been translated to him, 'there is an order from our headquarters about the matter. The British Army must not carry on any sale of metal on French soil.'

'Thank him very much,' said the colonel, satisfied.

'Now just look here,' he said to Barefoot on returning, 'what a nice mess you would have made if I hadn't known my business. Let this be a lesson to you. In future it will be better if you look after your men and leave the rest to me. As for the tins, I have thought of a solution which will satisfy everyone concerned.'

Next day Barefoot received orders to have the tins packed on lorries, and carried in several loads to the end of the pier, whence they were neatly cast into the sea. In this way the Mayor was spared the trouble of finding a dumping-ground, the British Government paid for the petrol consumed by the lorries, the *Ponts et Chaussées* bore the expense of the dredging, and, as Colonel Musgrave said, every one was satisfied.

Colonel Parker, before rejoining the Division, wrote out a report, as usual, about the operations at B——.

'I beg to draw attention,' the document ran, 'to the excellent organization of the Supply arrangements. Thirty thousand men have been provided with rations in a harbour where no British base existed. This result is due especially to the organizing abilities displayed by Colonel A. C. Musgrave, C.M.G., D.S.O. (R.A.S.C.). Although this officer has only recently been promoted, I consider it my duty to recommend him . . .'

'What about Barefoot?' said Aurelle. 'Couldn't he be made a captain?'

'Barefoot? That damned shop-keeper fellow whom Musgrave told me about? The man who wanted to introduce his methods into the army? He's a public danger, my boy! But I can propose your friend Major Baraquin for a C.M.G., if you like.'

'Baraquin?' Aurelle exclaimed in turn. 'Why, he always refused everything you asked him for.'

'Yes,' said the colonel; 'he's not very easy to get on with; he doesn't understand things; but he's a soldier, every inch of him! I like old Baraquin!'

CHAPTER V

THE STORY OF PRIVATE BIGGS

'La Nature fait peu de gens vaillants;
c'est la bonne institution et la discipline.'
CHARRON

The new padre was a stout, artless man with a kind face. He was only just out from England, and delighted the general with his air of innocent surprise.

'What's making all that noise?' he asked.

'Our guns,' said Colonel Parker.

'Really?' replied the padre, in mild astonishment. As he walked into the camp, he was stopped by a sentry.

'Who goes there?'

'Friend,' he answered. Then he went up to the man and added anxiously, 'I suppose that was the right thing to answer, wasn't it?'

The general was delighted at these stories, and asked the Rev. Mr Jeffries to take his meals at his own table.

'Padre,' he said, 'don't you think our Mess is a happy family?'

'Padre,' chimed in the doctor approvingly, 'don't you think that this Mess has all the characteristics of a family? It is just a group of people thrown together by chance, who never understand each other in the least, who criticize one another severely, and are compelled by circumstances to put up with each other.'

'There's nothing to joke about,' said Colonel Parker.

'It's these compulsory associations that often give rise to the finest devotion.'

And being in a lively mood that evening, he related the story of Private Biggs:

'You remember Biggs, who used to be my orderly? He was a shy, refined little fellow, who used to sell neckties in peace-time. He loathed war, shells, blood and danger.

'Well, at the end of 1916, the powers that be sent the battalion to Gamaches training camp. A training camp, padre, is a plot of ground traversed by imitation trenches, where officers who have never been near the line teach war-worn veterans their business.

'The officers in charge of these camps, having a *clientèle* to satisfy, start some new fashion every season. This spring I understand that "open file" is to be the order of the day; last autumn "massed formation" was the watchword of the best firms. There's a lot of talk been going on for some time, too, about "firing from the hip"; that's one of my friend Lamb's absolutely original creations—a clever fellow that; he ought to do very well.

'At Gamaches the officer in command was Major Macleod, a bloodthirsty Scot whose hobby was bayonet work. He was very successful at showing that, when all's said and done, it's the bayonet that wins battles. Others before him have sworn that it is only hand-grenades, heavy guns, or even cavalry that can give a decisive victory. But Macleod's doctrine was original in one respect: he favoured moral suggestion rather than actual practice for the manufacture of his soldiers. For the somewhat repulsive slaughter of bayonet fighting he found it necessary to inspire the men with a fierce hatred of the enemy.

'For this purpose he had bags of straw stuffed to the shape of German soldiers, adorned with a sort of German helmet and painted field-grey, and these were given as targets to our Highlanders.

' "Blood is flowing," he used to repeat as the training proceeded, "blood is flowing, and you must rejoice at the sight of it. Don't get tender-hearted; just think only of stabbing in the right place. To withdraw the bayonet from the corpse, place your foot on the stomach."

'You can imagine how Biggs's soul revolted at these speeches. In vain did Sergeant-Major Fairbanks of the Guards deliver himself of his most bloodthirsty *repertoire*; Biggs's tender heart was horror-struck at the idea of bowels and brains exposed, and it was always owing to him that the most carefully-prepared charges were deprived of the warlike frenzy demanded by Major Macleod.

' "*As* you were!" Sergeant-Major Fairbanks used to yell. "*As* you were! Now then, Private Biggs." And after twenty attempts had failed, he would conclude sadly. "Well, boys, mark my words, come Judgment Day, when we're all p'radin' for the final review an' the Lord comes along, no sooner will the Arch-angel give the order, ' 'Tention!' than 'e'll 'ave to shout, 'As you were! Now then, Private Biggs!' "

'When the period of training was over, Macleod assembled all our men in a large shed and gave 'em his celebrated lecture on "hatred of the enemy".

'I was really curious to hear him, because people at G.H.Q. were always talking about the extraordinary influence he had over the troops' *morale*. "One of Macleod's speeches," said the Chief of Staff, "does the Huns as much harm as ten batteries of heavy howitzers."

'The lecturer began with a ghastly description of the shooting of prisoners, and went on to a nauseating account of the effects of gas and a terrible story about the crucifixion of a Canadian sergeant; and then, when our flesh was creeping and our throats were dry, came a really eloquent hymn of hate, ending with an appeal to the avenging bayonet.

'Macleod was silent for a few minutes enjoying the sight of our haggard faces; then, considering we were sufficiently worked up, he went on:

' "Now, if there is any one of you who wants anything explained, let him speak up; I'm ready to answer any questions."

'Out of the silence came the still, small voice of Private Biggs.

' "Please, sir ?"

' "Yes, my man," said Major Macleod kindly.

' "Please, sir, can you tell me how I can transfer to the Army Service Corps ?"

'That evening, in the kitchen, our orderlies discussed the incident, and discovered in course of conversation that Biggs had never killed a man. All the others were tough old warriors, and they were much astonished.

'Kemble, the general's orderly, a giant with a dozen or so to his account, was full of pity for the poor little Cockney. "Mon, mon," he said, "I can hardly believe ye. Why, never a single one ? Not even wounded ?"

' "No," said Biggs, "honest Injun. I run so slowly, I'm always the last to get there—I never get a chance."

'Well, a few days later, the battalion was up in the line again, and was sent into a little stunt opposite Fleurbaix, to straighten out a salient. You remember, sir ? It's one of the best things the Division has ever done.

'Artillery preparation, low barrage, cutting communications—everything came off like clockwork, and we caught the Boches in their holes like rabbits.

'While the men were busy with their rifles, grenades and bayonets, cleaning up the conquered trenches, suddenly a voice was heard shouting:

' "Harry, Harry, where are you? . . . Just send Biggs along here, will you? . . . Pass the word along to Private Biggs."

'It was the voice of the Highlander, Kemble. Some giant grasped Biggs by the seat of his trousers and swung him and his rifle up to the parapet. Then two strong hands seized the little man, and he was swung in mid-air from man to man right up the file till he was finally handed over to Kemble, who seized him affectionately with his left hand, and, full of joy at the dainty treat he had in store for his friend, cried, "Mon, mon, look in this wee hole: I've got twa of 'em at the end of my rifle, but I've kept 'em for you."

'This is a true story,' added Colonel Parker, 'and it shows once more that the British soldier has a kind heart.'

The Rev. Mr Jeffries had turned very pale.

CHAPTER VI

AN AIR RAID

'I do not like seriousness. I think it is irreligious.'
CHESTERTON

'They'll be here soon,' said Dr O'Grady. 'The moon is low, and the shadows are long, and these oblique lights will suit them very well.'

The division was in rest on the hills overlooking Abbeville, and the doctor was walking to and fro with Colonel Parker and Aurelle along the lime-bordered terrace, from which they could see the town that was going to be attacked. From the wet grassy lawns near by groups of anxious women were scanning the horizon.

'Yesterday evening, in a suburb,' said Aurelle, 'they killed a baker's three children.'

'I am sorry,' put in the doctor, 'they should be favoured with this fine weather. The law of the storm seems to be exactly the same for these barbarians as it is for innocent birds. It's absolutely contradictory to the notion of a just Divinity.'

'Doctor,' said Aurelle, 'you are an unbeliever.'

'No,' replied the doctor, 'I am an Irishman, and I respect the bitter wisdom of the Catholic faith. But this universe of ours, I confess, strikes me as completely non-moral. Shells and decorations fall haphazard from above on the just and the unjust alike; M. Poincaré's carburettor gets out of order just as often as the Kaiser's.

The Gods have thrown up their job, and handed it over to the Fates. It is true that Apollo, who is a well-behaved person, takes out his chariot every morning; that may satisfy the poets and the astronomers, but it distresses the moralist. How satisfactory it would be if the resistance of the air were relative to the virtues of the airman, and if Archimedes' principle did not apply to pirates!'

'O'Grady,' observed Colonel Parker, 'you know the words of the psalm: "As for the ungodly, it is not so with them; but they are like the chaff which the wind scattereth away from the face of the earth."'

'Yes, colonel; but supposing you, a good man, and I, a sinner, were suddenly hit by a bomb——'

'But, doctor,' Aurelle interrupted, 'this science of yours is after all only an act of faith.'

'How so, my boy? It is obvious that there are laws in this world. If I press the trigger of this revolver, the bullet will fly out, and if General Webb is given an Army Corps, General Bramble will have a bilious attack.'

'Quite so, doctor; you observe a few series linked together, and you conclude that the world is governed by laws. But the most important facts—life, thought, love—elude your observations. You may perhaps be sure that the sun is going to rise tomorrow morning, but you don't know what Colonel Parker is going to say next minute. Yet you assert that the colonel is a machine; that is because your religion tells you to.'

'So does every one else's religion,' said the doctor. 'Only yesterday I read in the Bishop of Broadfield's message: "The prayers for rain cannot take place this week, as the barometer is too high."'

Far away over the plain, in the direction of Amiens,

the star-sprinkled sky began to flicker with tiny, flashing points of light.

'Here they come,' said Aurelle.

'They'll be ten minutes yet,' said the doctor. They resumed their walk.

'O'Grady,' Colonel Parker put in, 'you're getting more crazy every day. You claim, if I comprehend your foolish ideas aright, that a scientist can foretell rain better than an Anglican bishop. What a magnificent paradox! Meteorology and medicine are far less solid sciences than theology. *You* say that the universe is governed by laws, don't you? Nothing is less certain. It is true that chance seems to have established a relative balance in the tiny corner of the universe which we inhabit, but there is nothing to show that this balance is going to last. If you were to press the trigger of this revolver tomorrow, it is just possible that it would not go off. It is also possible that the German aeroplanes will cease to fly, and that General Bramble will take a dislike to the gramophone. *I* should not be surprised at any of these things; I should simply recognize that supernatural forces had come into our lives.'

'Doctor,' said Aurelle, 'you know the clock which my orderly Brommit winds up every evening? Let us suppose that on one of the molecules that go to make up the minute-hand of that clock there live a race of beings who are infinitely small, and yet as intelligent as we are. These little creatures have measured their world, and have noticed that the speed of its motion is constant; they have discovered that their planet covers a fixed distance in a fixed period of time, which for us is a minute and for them a century. Amongst their people there are two schools of thought. The scientists claim that the

laws of the universe are immutable, and that no supernatural power can intervene to change them. The
believers admit the existence of these laws, but they
also assert that there is a divine being who can interfere
with their course; and to that being they address prayers.
In that tiny world, which of them is right? The believers,
of course; for there is such a being as Private Brommit,
and if he forgets one evening to wind up the clock, the
scientists and all their proud theories will vanish away
like smoke in a cataclysm which will bring whole worlds
to their doom.'

'That's so,' said the doctor; 'but if they had
prayed——'

'Listen,' interrupted Aurelle.

The park had become strangely silent; and though
there was no wind, they could hear the gentle rustling
of the leaves, the barking of a dog in the valley, the
crackling of a twig under a bird's weight. Up above, in
the clear sky, there was a feeling of some hostile presence,
and a disagreeable little buzzing sound, as though there
were some invisible mosquito up among the stars.

'They're here now,' said the doctor.

The noise increased: a buzzing swarm of giant bees
seemed to be approaching the hill.

Suddenly there was a long hiss, and a ray of light
leaped forth from the valley and began to search the sky
with a sort of superhuman thoroughness. The women on
the lawn ran away to the shelter of the trees. The short,
sharp barking of the guns, the deeper rumble of the bombs
that were beginning to fall on the town, and the earth-
shaking explosions terrified them beyond endurance.

'I'm going to shut my eyes,' said one, 'it's easier like
that.'

'My God,' exclaimed another, 'I can't move my legs an inch!'

'Fear,' said the doctor, 'shows itself in hereditary reflexes. Man, when in danger, seeks the pack, and fright makes his flesh creep, because his furred ancestors bristled all over when in combat, in order to appear enormous and terrible.'

A terrific explosion shook the hill, and flames arose over the town.

'They're aiming at the station,' said the colonel. 'Those searchlights do more harm than good. They simply frame the target and show it up.'

'When I was at Le Havre,' Aurelle remarked, 'a gunner went to ask the Engineers for some searchlights that were rotting away in some store or other. "Quite impossible," said the engineer; "they're the war reserve; we're forbidden to touch them." He could never be brought to understand that the war we were carrying on over here was the one that was specified in his schedule.'

The great panting and throbbing of an aeroplane was coming nearer, and the whole sky was quivering with the noise of machinery like a huge factory.

'My God,' exclaimed the doctor, 'we're in for it this time!'

But the stars twinkled gently on, and above the din they heard the clear, delicate notes of a bird's song—just as though the throbbing motors, the whizzing shells and the frightened wailing of the women were nothing but the harmonies devised by the divine composer of some military-pastoral symphony to sustain the slender melody of a bird.

'Listen,' whispered Colonel Parker, 'listen—a nightingale!'

CHAPTER VII

LOVE AND THE INFANT DUNDAS

'. . . Of which, if thou be a severe sour-complexion'd man,
then I hereby disallow thee to be a competent judge.'
The Compleat Angler

The Infant Dundas struck up a rag-time on the sergeant-
major's typewriter, did a juggling turn with the army
list, and let forth a few hunting yells; then, seeing that
the interpreter had reached the required state of exas-
peration, he said:

'Aurelle, why should we stay in this camp? Let's go
into the town; I'll get hold of the Intelligence car, and
we'll go and see Germaine.'

Germaine was a pretty, friendly girl who sold novels,
chocolates and electric lamps at Abbeville. Dundas, who
was not interested in women, pretended to have a dis-
creet passion for her; in his mind France was associated
with the idea of love-affairs, and he thought it the right
thing to have a girl-friend there, just as he would have
thought it correct to hunt in Ireland, or to ski at St
Moritz.

But when Germaine, with feigned timidity, directed
on him the slowly dwindling fire of her gaze, Dundas
was afraid to put his arm round her waist; this rosy-
cheeked giant, who was a champion boxer and had
been wounded five times, was as bashful and shy as a
child.

'Good morning,' he would say with a blush.

'Good morning,' Germaine would answer, adding in a lower voice for Aurelle's benefit, 'Tell him to buy something.'

In vain did Aurelle endeavour to find books for the Infant. French novels bored him; only the elder Dumas and Alphonse Daudet found favour in his eyes. Dundas would buy his seventeenth electric lamp, stop a few minutes on the doorstep to play with Germaine's black dog Dick, and then say good-bye, giving her hand a long squeeze and going away perfectly happy in the thought that he had done his duty and gone on the spree in France in the correct manner.

'A nice boy, your friend—but he is rather shy,' she used to say.

On Sundays she went for walks along the river with an enormous mother and ungainly sisters, escorted gravely by Dundas. The mess did not approve of these rustic idylls.

'I saw him sitting beside her in a field,' said Colonel Parker, 'and his horse was tied to a tree. I think it's disgusting.'

'It's shameful,' said the padre.

'I'll speak to him about it,' said the general, 'it's a disgrace to the mess.'

Aurelle tried to speak up for his friend.

'Maybe,' said the doctor, 'pleasure is a right in France, but in England it's a crime. With you, Aurelle, when girls see you taking a lady-friend out, their opinion of you goes up. In London, on the other hand——'

'Do you mean to say, doctor, that the English never flirt?'

'They flirt more than you do, my boy; that's why

they say less about it. Austerity of doctrine bears a direct proportion to strength of instinct. You like to discuss these matters, because you think lightly of them, and in that we Irish resemble you. Our great writers, such as Bernard Shaw, write thousands of paradoxes about marriage, because their thoughts are chaste. The English are far more prudish because their passions are stronger.'

'What's all this you're saying, doctor?' interrupted the general. 'I seem to be hearing very strange doctrines.'

'We're talking about French morals, sir.'

'Is it true, Messiou,' inquired Colonel Parker, 'that it is the custom in France for a man to take his wife and his mistress to the theatre together to the same box?'

'You needn't try to convince Aurelle of your virtue, colonel,' said the doctor; 'he's been living with you for four years, and he knows you.'

Meanwhile Dundas continued to go down into Abbeville every day and meet his friend. The shelling had got very bad, and the inhabitants began to leave the town. Germaine, however, remained calm. One day a shell hit the shop next door to hers, and shattered the whole of the whitewashed front of the house, and the plaster crumbling away revealed a fine wooden building which for the last two centuries had been concealing its splendid carved beams beneath a wretched coat of whitewash. So also did Germaine, divested by danger of her superficial vulgarity, suddenly show her mettle and prove herself the daughter of a race of soldiers.

Accordingly Dundas had conceived a warm and respectful friendship for her. But he went no further until one day when the alarm caught them together just as he was bidding her good-bye; then only did the darkness and the pleasant excitement of danger cause him to forget ceremony and convention for a few minutes.

Next day Germaine presented the Infant with a fat yellow book; it was Madame de Stael's *Corinne*. The rosy-cheeked one looked askance at the small closely printed pages.

'Aurelle,' he implored, 'be a good chap and tell me what it's all about—I'm not going to read the damned thing!'

'It's the story of a young Scotch laird,' replied Aurelle, 'who wants to marry a foreign girl against his family's wish.'

'My God!' exclaimed Dundas. 'Do you think she expects me to marry her? My cousin Lord Bamford married a dancer and he's very happy; he's the gentleman and she has the brains. But in this case it's the mother—she's a terrible creature!'

'The Zulus,' put in the doctor, who was listening, 'have a religious custom which forbids the bridegroom-elect to see his mother-in-law. Should he happen but to see her footprints in the sand, he must turn and flee. Nothing could be wiser; for love implies an absurd and boundless admiration for the loved one, and her mother, appearing to the lover in the very image of his beloved without the charm and liveliness of youth, will deter him from that brief spell of folly which is so necessary for the propagation of the species.'

'Some mothers are charming,' argued Aurelle.

'That's another danger,' said the doctor, 'for as the mother always tends to live her daughter's emotional life, there is a constant risk of her falling in love with her son-in-law.'

'My God!' cried Dundas, horror-struck.

However, the German airmen set his fears at rest that very evening by destroying half the town. The statue of Admiral Courbet in the middle of the square near the bookseller's shop was hit by a bomb. The admiral continued to point an outstretched finger towards the station, but the bookseller cleared out. Germaine followed him regretfully.

As she was unable to take her dog Dick—a horrid mongrel, half-poodle and half-spaniel—Dundas gravely consented to look after him. He loved dogs with a sentimental warmth which he denied to men. Their ideas interested him, their philosophy was the same as his, and he used to talk to them for hours at a time like a nurse to her children.

The general and Colonel Parker were not a bit astonished when he introduced Dick into the mess. They had found fault with him for falling in love, but they approved of his adopting a dog.

Dick, an Abbeville guttersnipe, was therefore admitted to the refinements of the general's table. He remained, however, a rough son of the people, and barked when Private Brommit appeared with the meat.

'Behave yourself, sir,' Dundas said to him, genuinely shocked, 'behave yourself. A well-brought-up dog never, never does that. A good dog never barks indoors, never, never, never.'

Germaine's pet was offended and disappeared for three days. The orderlies reported he had been seen in the country in doubtful company. At last he returned, cheerful and unkempt, with one ear torn and one eye bleeding, and asked to be let in by barking merrily.

'You're a very naughty dog, sir,' said Dundas as he nursed him adroitly, 'a very, very bad little dog indeed.'

Whereupon he turned towards the general.

'I'm very much afraid, sir,' he said, 'that this fellow Dick is not quite a gentleman.'

'He's a French dog,' replied General Bramble with sorrowful forbearance.

CHAPTER VIII

A GREAT CHEF

'Le roi ordonnait le matin petit souper ou très petit souper; mais ce dernier était abondant et de trois services sans le fruit.'
SAINT-SIMON

In the month of February 1918, Aurelle was ordered by the French mission at British G.H.Q. to report at the *sous-préfecture* at Abbeville and to hold himself for one day at the disposal of M. Lucas, who would call for him in due course.

Aurelle waited for some time for M. Lucas, who eventually appeared escorted by an English chauffeur. He was a rather stout, clean-shaven little man, and wore a well-made blue suit and a yachting cap. With his hands in his pockets, his curt speech and the authority of his demeanour, he looked every inch a man accustomed to command.

'You are the interpreter from G.H.Q.?' he asked. 'Have you a written order?'

Aurelle was obliged to admit he had only received an order by telephone.

'I can't understand it!' said M. Lucas. 'The most necessary precautions are neglected. Have you at least been told who I am? No? Well, listen to me, my friend, and kindly hold your tongue for a minute.'

He went and shut the door of the *sous-préfet's* office, and came back to the interpreter. 'I am——' he began.

He looked nervously about him, closed a window, and whispered very softly, 'I am His Majesty the King of England's chef.'

'Chef?' Aurelle repeated, not grasping his meaning.

'His Majesty the King of England's chef,' the great man deigned to repeat, smiling kindly at the astonishment the young man showed at this revelation.

'You must know, my friend, that tomorrow the President of the Republic is to be His Majesty's guest in this town. The activity of the German airmen obliges us to keep the programme secret till the last moment. However, I have been sent out in advance with Sir Charles to inspect the British Officers' Club, where the lunch is to take place. You are to accompany me there.'

So they set off for the former Château de Vauclère, now transformed by British genius for comfort into an officers' club, Aurelle escorting the royal cook and the equerry, who was an old English gentleman with a pink face, white whiskers and grey spats. Above their heads circled the squadron of aeroplanes which had been ordered to protect the favoured city.

During the drive, M. Lucas condescended to say a few words of explanation.

'Our lunch is to be quite informal; the menu very simple—ever since the beginning of the war His Majesty has expressed a wish to be rationed like his people— river trout, *tournedos aux pommes*, some fruit, and cider to drink.'

'But, Monsieur Lucas,' interrupted Sir Charles timidly, 'you know Her Majesty prefers to drink milk.'

'The Queen will drink cider like every one else,' replied the chef curtly.

Sir Charles was charmed with the paved courtyard of

the château, the brick and stone façade with its carved escutcheons, the simple curves of the dining-room panelling, and the picture over the door, which he attributed, not without reason, to Nattier.

'It's very, very small,' murmured M. Lucas pensively. 'However, as it's wartime——'

Then he inquired about the kitchen. It was a vast and well-lighted place; the red and white tiles on the polished floor shone brightly in the sunshine; magnificent but useless copper saucepans hung upon the walls.

In front of the oven a cook in a white cap was at work with a few assistants. Surprised by the noise, he turned round, and, suddenly recognizing the man in the blue suit, went as white as his cap, and dropped the pan he was holding in his hand.

'You ?' he exclaimed.

'Yes, my friend,' replied the august visitor quite simply. 'What a surprise to find you here! What a pleasure also,' he added kindly. 'Ah, now I feel relieved! An alfresco meal, a strange kitchen like this, made me very anxious, I must confess. But with such a lieutenant as you, my dear friend, the battle is already half won.'

'Yes,' he continued, turning towards Aurelle, who was gazing with emotion upon the encounter and thinking of Napoleon entrusting his cavalry to Ney on the eve of Waterloo, 'it is a curious coincidence to find Jean Paillard here. At the age of fifteen we made our *début* together under the great Escoffier. When I was appointed chef to the Ritz, Paillard took charge of the Carlton; when I took Westminster, he accepted Norfolk.'

Having thus unconsciously delivered himself of this romantic couplet—which goes to prove once again that poetry is the ancient and natural expression of all true feeling—M. Lucas paused for a moment, and, lowering his gaze, added in an infinitely expressive undertone:

'And here I am now with the King. What about you?'

'I?' replied the other with a touch of shame. 'It's only two months since I was released; till then I was in the trenches.'

'What!' exclaimed M. Lucas, scandalized. 'In the trenches? A chef like you!'

'Yes,' answered Jean Paillard with dignity. 'I was cook at G.H.Q.'

With a shrug of resignation the two artists deplored the waste of talent for which armed democracies are responsible; and M. Lucas began in resolute tones to announce his plan of campaign. He had the curt precision which all great captains possess.

'Since the war broke out, His Majesty has expressed a wish to be rationed like his people. Therefore the menu is to be very simple: *truite à la Bellevue, tournedos aux pommes*, some fruit.—Of course there will have to be an entrée and some dessert for the Staff. The drink will be cider.'

'May I remind you, Monsieur Lucas,' Sir Charles put in anxiously, 'that Her Majesty prefers to drink milk?'

'I have already told you,' said the chef, annoyed, 'that the Queen will drink cider like everybody else. . . . Nevertheless, Paillard, you will kindly show me the contents of your cellar; there will, of course, have to be wine for the Staff. The *tournedos*, I need hardly say, are to be grilled over a charcoal fire, and larded, of course. As to salad—seasoning, tomatoes and walnuts——'

As he gave his orders, he illustrated their execution

with gestures of the utmost solemnity, and his hands moved busily amongst imaginary saucepans.

'The menu is short,' he said, 'but it must be perfect. The great cook is better recognized by the perfection of a piece of beef—or let me say rather by the seasoning of a salad—than by the richness of his sweets. One of the finest successes in my career—the one I enjoy recalling above all others—is that of having initiated the English aristocracy into the mysteries of Camembert. The choice of fruit—now I come to think of it, Paillard, have you any peaches?'

'I should think we had!' said the latter, breaking open the lid of a crate which revealed a number of delicately shaded ripe peaches glowing in their beds of straw and cotton-wool.

The chef took one and stroked it gently.

'Paillard, Paillard,' he said sadly, 'do you call *these* peaches? I can see you have been a soldier, poor fellow. Never mind, I can send the car to Montreuil.'

He remained a few minutes longer in meditation; then, satisfied at last, he decided to leave the château. In the street, he took Aurelle's arm very kindly.

'My friend,' he said, 'I think that will do, thank you. And if you ever have the opportunity of seeing Their Majesties, don't let it slip by. In France, you have very wrong ideas, I assure you; since the Revolution, you have a prejudice against Royal Families. It is childish; you can take my word for it. I have been living with this one for more than five years, and I assure you they are quite respectable people.'

CHAPTER IX

PRÉLUDE À LA SOIRÉE D'UN GÉNÉRAL

'. . . of cabbages and kings.'
LEWIS CARROLL

A blue forage-cap appeared under the flap of the camou-flaged tent.

'Messiou,' cried the general, 'we were beginning to despair of ever seeing you again.'

'Yo-ho! Hello—o!' shouted the Infant Dundas. 'I *am* glad! Come and have some lunch, old man.'

Aurelle, happy to find his friends again, fell to heartily on the mutton, boiled potatoes and mint sauce. When they reached the cheese, General Bramble questioned him about his journey.

'Well, Messiou, what about your leave? What is Paris looking like nowadays, and why did your mother the French Mission tell us she was keeping you two days at Abbeville?'

Aurelle told them the story of M. Lucas and of the King's visit.

'What's that, Messiou?' said General Bramble. 'You've seen our King? Does he look well?'

'Very well indeed, sir.'

'Good old George!' muttered the general tenderly. 'Yes, he looked quite well when he came here. Tell us that story of the cook over again, Messiou; it's a jolly good story.'

Aurelle complied, and when he had done, he bent

over towards Colonel Parker and asked him why the general spoke of the King like an affectionate nurse.

'The King,' said the colonel, 'is much more to us than you might imagine. To the general, who is an Etonian, he is a kind of neighbour. To Dundas, he's the colonel of his regiment. To the padre, he's the head of the Church. To an old Tory like me, he's the living embodiment of England's traditions and prejudices, and the pledge of her loyalty to them in the future. As for the paternal tone, that's because for half a century the King was a Queen. Loyalism became an attitude of protective chivalry; nothing could have consolidated the dynasty more firmly. Royalty is beloved not only by the aristocracy but by all classes. It's a great asset to a people without imagination like ours to be able to see in one man the embodiment of the nation.'

'Messiou,' interposed the general, 'didn't they give you an M.V.O. for your services?'

'What is that, sir—a new ribbon?'

'My God!' exclaimed Dundas, much scandalized. 'You've never heard of the Victorian Order?'

'When King Edward played bridge,' said the general, 'and his partner left it to him at the right moment, the King used to declare with great satisfaction, "No trumps, and you're an M.V.O.!"'

'The idea that a word from the sovereign's lips or the contact of his person is sufficient to cure his subjects, is a very ancient and beautiful one,' said the colonel. 'Before he started distributing ribbons, the King used to cure scrofula. That excellent custom, however, came to an end with William of Orange, who used to say to the patient while he was operating, "God give you better health and more sense!"'

'The King's taboo has also disappeared,' said the doctor.

'I can assure you,' said Aurelle, 'that his taboo is still effective. On the platform before he arrived there were three A.P.M.'s bustling about and chasing away the few spectators. As the train came into the station one of them ran up to me and said, "Are you the interpreter on duty? Well, there's a seedy-looking chap over there, who seems up to no good. Go and tell him from me that if he doesn't clear out immediately I'll have him arrested." I did so. "Arrest me!" said the man. "Why, I'm the special *commissaire de police* entrusted with the King's safety." '

'Well, Messiou,' inquired the general, 'have you brought me back any new records from Paris for my gramophone?'

Aurelle unstrapped his kit and proceeded, not without some anxiety, to unpack 'Le Prélude à l'Après-midi d'un Faune.'

'I don't know whether you'll like it, sir; it's modern French music.'

'I'm sure it's very fine, Messiou,' said the general confidently. And in the interest of international courtesy he immediately assumed the beatific expression he usually kept for Caruso.

After the first few notes, an air of bewilderment appeared upon his kindly face. He looked at Aurelle, whom he was surprised to find quite unmoved; at Colonel Parker, who was hard at work; at the doctor, who was inclining his head and listening devoutly; and, resigning himself to his fate, he waited for the end of the acidulated and discordant noises.

'Well, Messiou,' he said when it was over, 'it's very nice of you not to have forgotten us—but——'

'Yes,' put in Colonel Parker, looking up, 'but I'm damned if it's music!'

'What?' shouted the doctor, scandalized. 'A masterpiece like that? Not music?'

'Come, come,' said the general soothingly, 'maybe it wasn't written for the gramophone. But, doctor, I should like you to explain.'

'Have you seen the Russian Ballet, sir? The faun, lying on a rock, is watching for the nymphs and playing in a monotonous key on his flute. At last they appear, half dressed; he pursues them, but they fly away, and one of them drops a sash, which is all he gets.'

'This is very interesting,' said the general, much excited. 'Wind up the gramophone, Messiou, and give us the disc over again; I want to see the half-dressed nymphs. Make a sign to me at the right moment.'

Once again the instrument filled the rustic dug-out with the wistful grace of the Prelude. Aurelle murmured in a low voice:

> *'Ces nymphes, je les veaux perpétuer, si clair*
> *Leur incarnat léger qu'il voltige dans l'air*
> *Assoupi de sommeils touffus. . . .'*

'Bravo, Messiou!' said the general, when the last notes rang out. 'I like it better already than I did the first time. I'm sure I'll get used to it in the end.'

'I shan't,' said Colonel Parker. 'I shall always prefer "God Save the King".'

'Yes,' replied the doctor; 'but your children will hum "Pelléas," and your grandchildren will say, "Do you know that old tune that used to be the rage in grand-father's time?" What you never can get used to, colonel, is finding yourself in the presence of a somewhat more complex work of art than the childish productions to which you are accustomed. Nature is not simple; she takes the theme of a fox-trot and makes a funeral march out of it; and it is just these incongruities that are the essence of all poetry. I appeal to you for an opinion, Aurelle, as a citizen of the country which has produced Debussy and Mallarmé.'

'Have you ever heard the excellent saying of Renoir, the old French painter: "Don't ask *me*," he said, "whether painting ought to be subjective or objective; I confess I don't care a rap." '

'Ah, Messiou,' sighed the general, 'the confounded fellow was quite right too!'

CHAPTER X

PRIVATE BROMMIT'S CONVERSION

> 'Paris vaut bien une messe.'
> HENRI IV

Aurelle was wakened every morning by Colonel Parker's orderly, a tough, thick-set, astute old soldier, who expounded the unwritten laws of the army for the benefit of the young Frenchman as he dexterously folded his clothes.

'You know, sir,' he said, 'as 'ow the British Tommy 'as to go to church in peace-time every blessed Sunday. When the time for p'rade comes along, the orficer on dooty gives the order to fall in accordin' to religions, an' the Church of England men, an' the Presbyterians an' the Cath'lics is marched up to their services, rifles an' all.

'The orficer takes charge of one of the detachments, an' in the others the senior N.C.O. for each religion marches at the head. Wotever dodge you try on, there's no gettin' out of it.

'When once you've gone an' accepted the King's shillin', it stands to reason you've got to put up with lots o' things, but Church P'rade's *the* very limit. Don't you take me for a 'eathen, sir; I'm much more of a believer than 'eaps of others. I don't mind singin' 'ymns, an' when the preacher can talk a bit, I don't objeck to sermons. But what used to get on my nerves was the cleanin' up Sunday mornin's. You've only seen us in khaki; you don't know our peace-time church togs. Some blasted togs they were too, an' no mistake—all glitterin' with blinkin' red an' gold, an' covered with white beltin'. An' the inspection before you start wasn't no joke, I can tell you. Many's the weeks' pay I've 'ad stopped, all on account of Sunday mornin's. I'm a pretty good soldier on active service, sir—why, you seen me at Loos, didn't you?—but what I can't stick is all them barricks an' fatigues an' cleanin' ups.

'F'r a long time I used to say to myself, "Brommit, my boy, you're a blasted idiot—I can understand a young rookie with only two or three years' service not managin' to get out of Church P'rade, but a soldier of fifteen years' standin' ought to know the tricks of the trade by this time. If *you* can't manage to stop quietly in bed on Sunday mornin's, you ain't worth yer service stripes," I says.

'But the more I thought about it the more 'opeless it seemed. Our colonel was old W. J. Reid—Slippery Bill we used to call 'im, 'cos 'e was as slippery as a soapy plank! 'E *was* an old monkey-face, an' no mistake.

'One day I was called up to the orderly-room to sign somethin' or other, an' I sees a poster on the wall: "Classification according to religions"—neat little chart it was: "Church of England, so many—Presbyterians, so many—Catholics, so many." You bet I didn't pay much attention to the numbers. Wot caught my eye was a column saying', "Wesleyans, None." An' all of a sudden I saw my game.

' "Wesleyans, None." So there wasn't even a bloomin' Wesleyan N.C.O. to take what Wesleyans there might be to chapel! Probably there wasn't even one bloomin' Wesleyan minister in the little Irish town where we was billeted. I saw myself at last stayin' in bed every blessed Sunday mornin'. At the very worst, if that there little religion 'ad a chapel, I'd be sent there on my own, and a detachment of one can always be trusted to find its way about. Wesleyan—that was the winner.

'Still, I 'ad one anxiety to 'old me back: I didn't for the life of me know what that there fancy religion might be. I'm not exactly a pious bloke, but I'm a good Christian, an' I didn't want to make a damned idiot o' myself. Besides, it would probably be a serious matter, I thought, to change your religion in the army. P'r'aps I'd 'ave to see old Bill 'imself about it, an' Bill wasn't exactly one of them fellers you can take in with some 'arf-baked tale.

'It was no good trying to get to know anythink in barracks. I'd only 'ave attracted notice at an awkward moment. But I knew a girl in the town as knew people 'oo knowed, so I asked 'er to make inquiries.

'She gave me an A1 character. An' blowed if I 'adn't been 'an found quite a decent religion; it suited me down to the ground. O' course you know 'oo Wesley was, sir? 'E was a feller as thought that bishops an' chaplains in 'is time didn't act accordin' to Scripture. 'E preached the return to poverty an' 'umbleness an' love of one's neighbour. You bet the Church of England couldn't swallow that! On the 'ole it was an 'onest kind of religion, an' a decent chap like me might very well 'ave gone in for it without its appearin' too out o' the way.

'Well, when I'd got myself well primed up about old Wesley, I felt as 'ow a little interview with Bill wasn't such a terrible thing after all. So I goes to see the sergeant-major, and tells 'im I wants to speak to the colonel.

' "Wot about?" 'e asks.

' "Strickly privit," I says.

' 'E'd 'ave liked to 'ave got my story out 'o me then an' there, 'e would, but I knew my only chance was to take Bill off 'is guard, so I kep' the secret of my plan of attack.

' "Well, Brommit," says the old man quite pleasant like, "have you got any complaint to make?"

' "No complaints, sir," says I; "everything's O.K. But I've asked leave to speak to you, 'cos I wanted to tell you, sir, as 'ow I intend to change my religion."

'I saw I'd got old Bill set for once, an' no mistake.

' "Change your religion?" 'e says. "Stuff and nonsense! Have you ever heard of such a thing, sergeant-major? What's your religion at present?"

' "Church of England, sir; but I wish to be put down in future as Wesleyan."

' "Well, I'm——! Who on earth put that notion into your head, my man? Has the padre offended you, or what?"

' "Oh no, sir, not at all; on the contrary, Mr Morrison's always been very kind to me. No, it ain't that at all, sir; but I don't believe in the Church of England no more, that's all."

' "You don't believe any more . . .? What don't you believe? What do *you* know about beliefs and dogmas?"

' "Why, sir, lots o' things," I says. "F'r instance, there's the bishops; I don't 'old with their way of livin', sir."

' "By Jove, sergeant-major, do you hear this damned idiot? He doesn't hold with the bishops' way of living! May I ask, Brommit, where you have had occasion to observe the ways of bishops?"

' "Well, sir, Wesley was a splendid fellow . . ." An' off I starts to spit out everythink my girl 'ad managed to get 'old of, without lettin' 'im put in a word. You bet 'e'd 'ad enough of it after five minutes. 'E'd 'ave liked to shut me up, but 'e couldn't do that without grantin' me wot I was askin' for. There was no flies on *my* conversion, I can tell you; I 'ad real live scruples; I'd been thinkin' too much. You can't punish a chap becos 'e thinks too much.

'The old man knew 'is job as well as I knew mine. 'E saw at once 'e only 'ad one thing to do.

' "All right," 'e said "After all, it's your own affair, my man. Sergeant-major, put him down as a Wesleyan. Brommit, you will come back to my room on Friday evening, and meanwhile I will arrange matters with the Wesleyan minister so that you can attend the services. You know where he lives, of course?"

' "No, sir, I don't know 'im."

' "That's rather strange. Well, never mind, I'll find him. Come back on Friday, Brommit."

'Slippery old Bill! 'E knew a thing or two, 'e did! Next Friday evenin', when I went up to 'im, 'e says:

' "Ah! I've settled everything," says 'e. "I've seen the Wesleyan minister, the Rev. Mr Short. A charming man, Mr Short. It's settled with him that you're to go to chapel on Sunday mornings at nine and on Sunday evenings at six. Yes, there are two services; Wesleyans are very strict. Of course if by any chance you miss a service, Mr Short is sure to let me know, and I would take the necessary steps. But there's no need to think of that, is there? A man who takes the trouble to change his religion at the age of thirty is hardly likely to miss a service. So that's all right, Brommit."

'Oh, damn cute 'e was, was Slippery Bill! Next Sunday off I goes to the Reverend Short's chapel. Tall, lean chap 'e was, with a real wicked face. 'E gave us an awful sermon all about 'ow we were to reform our lives, an' about all the things we was to renounce in this world, an' about the 'orrible fire as was awaitin' us in the next if we didn't follow 'is advice. After the service Mr Short comes up to me an' asks me to stay on after the others. Blowed if 'e didn't keep me till twelve o'clock jawin' me about the dooties my noo faith brought me an' about wot I read an' 'oo I talked to. By the time I got away from 'im I was 'arf stunned; an' I 'ad to go again in the evenin'!

'Every blinkin' Sunday the same thing 'appened. I used to spend the 'ole week swearin' and sendin' Short an' Wesley to the 'ottest place in the world. Once I tried on not goin' to chapel; but the miserable old 'ound split on me to the colonel, an' I 'ad a week's pay stopped. Then that there blessed Congregation invented Friday evenin' lectures; and the converted soldier, sent by kind permission of the colonel, was the finest ornament they 'ad.

'Well, wot put an end to my patience was a month later, when Short 'ad the cheek to jaw me personally about the girl I was walkin' out with. I went clean mad then, an' was ready for anythink, even for 'avin' it out again with Bill, rather than put up with that maniac's talk.

' "Please, sir," I tells the colonel, "I'm sorry to trouble you again with my religion, but this 'ere Wesleyanism don't satisfy me at all. It ain't a bit wot I'd 'oped for."

'I expected to get jolly well strafed, but I didn't. Bill just looked at me with a smile.

' "That's all right, Brommit," 'e said; "the Government pays me for looking after the moral health of my men. And may I inquire what religion is at present enjoying the favour of your approval?"

' "Well, sir, I don't see none at all. I've made myself a sort o' religion o' my own—if you'll allow it, of course."

' "I? Why, it's none of *my* business, Brommit. On the contrary, I admire the vitality of your mind. You've evidently got beliefs of your own; that's a very good sign indeed. It's just that they will not admit the obligation of going to a place of public worship on a Sunday, that's all. I presume I am taking you correctly?"

' "Yes, sir, quite correctly."

' "What an admirable coincidence, Brommit! For a long time I've been looking for somebody to scrub the stairs thoroughly on Sundays, while the men are at church. Sergeant-major, put Brommit down as an Agnostic—on permanent fatigue for scrubbing the stairs on Sunday mornings." '

CHAPTER XI

JUSTICE

The D.M.S. had sent round a note to all A.D.M.S.'s reminding them that all officers and men were to be inoculated against typhoid fever. So the A.D.M.S. of the Scottish Division ordered the different units to send in a nominal roll of all those who had not been inoculated. Most of the negligent confessed their sin; many of them were believers, and those who were not, respected the customs of their times and piously submitted to the ceremony.

Only the 113th Battery, R.F.A., sent in the following roll:

Names.	Condition.	Reason given for exemption.
Capt. Cockell . . Lieut. Little . : Lieut. M'Cracken .	Not yet inoculated. Refuse inoculation.	Do not believe in the efficacy of the operation.

The A.D.M.S. in high dudgeon complained to the Staff and requested the temporal powers to deliver the heretics over to the lancet. The temporal powers, while paying due reverence to medical infallibility, requested the A.D.M.S. to attempt a conversion.

The 113th Battery was famous for its courage and its daring deeds. Dr O'Grady was entrusted with the mission of visiting Captain Cockell and bringing that erring soul back to the fold.

The gunners gave the doctor a warm welcome. Their dug-out was comfortable, their arm-chairs, made by the men out of the branches of fir-trees, were luxuriously low and deep. O'Grady dropped into one, and looked about him anxiously.

'It is a remarkable fact,' he said, 'that thirst and hunger should make themselves felt by sensations in the mouth and stomach only, and not in the rest of the body. At this very moment, when all my organs are quite dry for lack of decent whisky, I am only warned by the mucous membrane in my mouth——'

'Orderly! The whisky! Quick!' shouted Captain Cockell.

Whereupon the doctor, his mind set at rest, was able to explain the object of his mission.

'Doctor,' answered Captain Cockell, 'there is nothing I would not do for you. But I consider anti-typhoid inoculation, next to poison-gas, to be the most dangerous practice in this war.'

The doctor, who was a skilful reader of character, saw at once that only liberal doctrines would help him to success.

'Oh,' he exclaimed genially, 'you needn't think I share the usual medical superstitions. But I do believe that inoculation has practically done away with deaths caused by typhoid. Statistics show——'

'Doctor, you know as well as I do that statistics may be made to say anything one likes. There are fewer cases of typhoid in this war than in former wars simply because the general sanitary conditions are much better. Besides, when a fellow who has been inoculated is silly enough to be ill—and that *has* been known to occur—you simply say, "It isn't typhoid—it's para-typhoid." '

'Which is perfectly true,' said the doctor; 'the pseudo-bacillus——'

'Oh, that stunt about the pseudo-bacillus! Next time you're wounded, doctor, I'll say it was by a pseudo-shell!'

'Very well, very well,' said the doctor, somewhat nettled. 'I'll just wait till next time you're ill. Then we'll see whether you despise doctors or not.'

'That's a poor argument, doctor, very poor indeed. I'm quite ready to acknowledge that a sick man is in need of moral support and requires the illusion of a remedy, just like a woman in love. Therefore doctors are necessary, just like thought-readers. I simply submit it should be recognized that both professions are of a similar order.'

The energetic Cockell had inspired his two young lieutenants with respectful admiration. They remained as firm as he in their refusal; and after an excellent lunch Dr O'Grady returned to H.Q. and informed his chief of the cynicism of the 113th Battery and the obstinacy of the heretical sect in those parts.

The A.D.M.S. sent the names of the three officers up to H.Q., and demanded the general's authority to put a stop to this scandal; and Colonel Parker promised to let the Corps know of the matter.

Some time before this, the French Government had placed at the disposal of the British authorities a certain number of 'Legion of Honour' decorations—to wit, two Grand Officer's badges, twelve Commander's cravats, twenty-four Officer's rosettes, and a considerable number of Knight's crosses.

The two Governments were in the habit of exchanging armfuls of ribbons at regular intervals in this way, and the apportioning of these trifles created a useful occupation for the numerous members of all staffs and their still more numerous clerks.

The distribution was performed according to wisely appointed rules. Of each batch of decorations G.H.Q. took one half for its own members, and passed on the other half to the Army Staffs. The Army Staffs kept half of what they received, and passed on the remainder to the Corps Staffs. The same method was applied right down to the Battalion Staffs, and it will readily be observed (with the help of an elementary arithmetical calculation) that the likelihood of the men in the line ever receiving a foreign decoration was practically non-existent.

The Scottish Division received as its share on this occasion three crosses. Colonel Parker and the other demi-gods of the divisional Olympus being already provided for, these were allotted to dignitaries of minor importance. It was decided that one should be given to Dr O'Grady, who had done great service to the French population (he had assisted a Belgian refugee in childbirth and she had survived his ministrations). The second was marked down for the D.A.D.O.S., and the third for the A.D.V.S., a genial fellow who was very popular in the mess.

The names of the three lucky men were handed by a Staff officer to an intelligent clerk with orders to draw up immediately a set of nominal rolls for the Corps.

Unfortunately the clerk happened to be the very same man to whom Colonel Parker had given the list of the three heretics of the 113th Battery the day before. But who can blame him for having confused two groups of three names? And who can blame the officer on duty for having signed two nominal rolls without reading them?

A month later, the Division was surprised to hear that Captain Cockell and Lieutenants Little and M'Cracken had been made Knights of the Legion of Honour. As they really deserved it, the choice caused considerable astonishment and general rejoicing; and the three warriors, happy to see three decorations reach them intact after having passed through so many covetous hands, were loud in praise of their superior officers' discrimination.

CHAPTER XII

VARIATIONS

'I have no illusions left but the Archbishop of Canterbury.'
SYDNEY SMITH

'When I was attached to a field-ambulance,' said the doctor, 'we had three padres with us in the mess.'

'That was rather a large order,' said the Rev. Mr Jeffries.

'It *was* a large order,' agreed the doctor, 'but one of them anyway was quite harmless. The R.C. padre spoke very little, ate an enormous amount, and listened with infinite contempt to the discussions of his colleagues.

'I don't want to hurt your feelings padre, but Catholicism is *the* only religion. A faith is only justified if it carries conviction. What's the use of a creed or a dogma which is as transient as a philosophy? Being condemned by my profession to study beings whose moral balance is unstable, I am in a position to assert that the Roman Church has a complete understanding of human nature. As a psychologist and a doctor, I admire the uncompromising attitude of the Councils. So much weakness and stupidity requires the firm support of an authority without the slightest tolerance. The curative value of a doctrine lies not in its logical truth, but in its permanency.'

'It is quite true,' said Colonel Parker, 'that nothing short of the rigid dictates of Catholicism could have prevented the Irish from going completely mad. But don't judge every one from your own case, O'Grady; the Saxons possess a solid, Protestant intelligence.'

'Well,' the doctor continued, 'our other two padres spent their evenings trying to swallow each other up. One of them was Church of England and the other Presbyterian; and they employed the most modern commercial methods in their competition. Church of England found an old gipsy cart which he set up at Dickebusch and from which he sold chocolate to the Jocks; whereupon Church of Scotland installed a telescope at Kruystraete to show them the stars. If the one formed a cigar-trust, the other made a corner in cigarettes. If one of them introduced a magic lantern, the other chartered a cinema. But the permanent threat to the peace of the mess was undoubtedly the Baptist question.

'As we had no Baptist padre, the unfortunate soldiers of that persuasion (of whom there were seven in the Division) could attend no service. The astonishing thing was that they never seemed to realize the extent of their misfortune.

'On one point at any rate our two padres agreed: men could not be left, in the dangerous zone in which we were then living, without the consolations of religion. But both Church of England and Church of Scotland each claimed the right to annex this tiny neutral congregation.

' "Excuse me," said Church of Scotland; "the Baptist, it is true, only performs the immersion ceremony when the adult's faith is confirmed, but on all other points he resembles the Presbyterian. His Church is a democratic one and is opposed to episcopacy, like ours."

' "Pardon me," said Church of England; "the Baptist,

in demanding a return to the primitive form of the Sacrament, proves himself to be the most conservative of all British Christians. Now every one—including yourself—admits that the Church of England is the most conservative of all the Reformed Churches. Besides——"

'For hours at a time they used to go on like this, and the futile discussion became even more annoying as I got to know the different arguments as well as either of them.

'One day I was sent up to the ambulance's advance post at Maple Copse—you know, that little wood in front of Ypres.'

'Unhealthy spot that,' said the general.

'So unhealthy, sir, that while I was there a whizz-bang hit my dug-out and blew my sergeant into small pieces, which remained hanging on the branches of the trees. It was a pity, for he was the best forward in the brigade football team. I put all I could find of him into a cloth, announced the burial for the next day, and then, as it was my turn to be relieved, I went back to the ambulance headquarters.

'My return was distinctly lively. On leaving the splendid trench which is called Zillebeke Road, I was silly enough to cross the exposed ground near the railway embankment. A machine-gun thought it rather amusing to have a pot at me from Hill 60——'

'All right, doctor,' said General Bramble, 'spare us the details.'

'Well, just as I left Ypres, I came across a Ford car which took me back to camp. In the mess I found Church of England and Church of Scotland arguing away as usual, while Roman Church was reading his breviary in a corner.

' "Satan, whence comest thou?" one of them asked me.

' "Well, gentlemen," I replied, "you ought to be glad to see me, because I really am back from hell this time."

'And I told them my adventures, putting in a lot of local colour about cannonades, explosions, whistling bullets and hailstorm barrages, in a style worthy of our best war correspondents.'

'You old humbug!' grunted the colonel.

' "By the way," I concluded, "I've got a job for one of you! Freshwater, my sergeant, has been blown to bits, and what I could collect of him is to be buried tomorrow morning. I'll give you the route—Messines gate, Zille-beke——"

'I saw the two padres' faces fall swiftly.

' "What religion?" they both asked simultaneously.

' "Baptist," I replied carelessly. "Have a cigarette, padre?"

'The two enemies gazed attentively at the ceiling; Roman Church kept his nose in his breviary and his ears well pricked up.

' "Well," said Church of England at length, "I wouldn't mind going up to Zillebeke. I've been in worse places to bury a man of my own Church. But for a Baptist it strikes me, O'Grady——"

' "Excuse me," interrupted Church of Scotland. "Baptism is the most conservative form of British Christianity, and the Anglican Church itself boasts——'

' "I dare say, I dare say," said the other, "but is not the Baptist Church a democratic one, like the Pres-byterian?"

'They might have gone on in this strain till the poor beggar was in his grave, had not the Roman Church suddenly interrupted in a mild voice, without taking his nose out of his little book:

' "I'll go, if you like."

'Hatred of Popery is the beginning of union, and they both went up the line together.'

CHAPTER XIII

THE CURE

'Le *Schein* et le *Wesen* sont, pour l'esprit
allemand, une seule et même chose.'
                JACQUES RIVIÈRE

'The only decent whisky,' said the doctor, 'is Irish
whisky.' Whereupon he helped himself to a generous
allowance of Scotch whisky, and as they had just been
talking about Ludendorff's coming offensive, he began
to discourse upon the Germans.

'One of the most astounding things about German
psychology,' he said, 'is their passion for suggesting the
appearance of results which they know they are power-
less to attain. A German general who is not in a position to
undertake a real offensive deludes himself into believing
that he will strike terror into his opponent by describing
an absurd and appalling attack in his reports; and a
Solingen cutler, if he cannot manufacture really sharp
blades at the required price, will endeavour to invoke a
sort of metaphysical blade which can give its owner the
illusion of a useful instrument.

'When once this trait of the national character is
properly understood, all the German shoddy which is
so much talked about seems no longer the swindling
practice of dishonest tradesmen, but is simply the material
expression of their ingrained Kantianism, and their
congenital inability to distinguish Appearance from
Reality.

H*   [229]

'At the sanatorium at Wiesdorf, where I was working when the war broke out, this method was practised with quite unusual rigour.

'Doctor Professor Baron von Göteburg was a second-rate scientist, and he knew it. He had made a lifelong study of the expression, clothes and manners which would most successfully impress his clients with the idea that he was the great physician he knew he could never be.

'After innumerable careful experiments, which do him the greatest credit, he had decided on a pointed beard, a military expression, a frock coat and a baron's title.

'Everything in his admirable establishment bore the impress of the kind of scientific precision which is the most striking hall-mark of ignorance. The Wiesdorf sanatorium extracted from the human carcase the maximum amount of formulæ, scientific jargon and professional fees which it could possibly yield. The patients felt themselves surrounded by a pleasant and luxurious apparatus of diagnoses, figures and diagrams.

'Each patient had a suite of rooms furnished, in spite of a rather obvious Munich atmosphere, with a sense of real comfort and order. Each floor was under the supervision of a doctor, a lean, athletic Swedish *masseur* and a qualified nurse in a white apron. The nurses were nearly all daughters of the nobility, whose happiness had been sacrificed to the extravagance of their brothers, who were generally captains in the Guards. The one attached to the floor I was in charge of was a French Alsatian with an innocent, obstinate face, whom the Germans called "Schwester Therese", and who asked me to call her "Sœur Thérèse".

'The place was only opened in the spring of 1914, and from the very first season its success had testified to the excellence of the system. Photographs were published in all the fashionable papers, and wealthy clients rushed in with alarming and automatic rapidity.

'On my floor I had an old American, one James P. Griffith, an English lady, the Duchess of Broadfield, and a Russian, Princess Uriassof. None of these three patients displayed symptoms of any illness whatsoever; they just complained of depression—nothing could amuse them—and of an appetite which no dish could tempt. When the American arrived, I considered it my duty to inform the professor of the excellent health in which I found him.

' "O'Grady," he said, staring hard at me with his brilliant, commanding eyes, "kindly give yourself less trouble. Your patient is suffering from congestion of the purse, and I think we shall be able to give him some relief."

'The Duchess of Broadfield longed to put on flesh, and wept all day long. "Madam," Sister Therese said to her, "if you want to get stouter, you ought to try and enjoy yourself." That caused a nice scene! I was obliged to explain to the nurse that the Duchess was on no account to be spoken to before eleven in the morning, and that it was improper to address her without calling her "Your Grace"!

'As to Princess Uriassof, she had been preceded by a courier, who had burst into indignant exclamations at the sight of the Munich furniture and had demanded genuine antiques. The professor smiled, and summoned a furniture dealer and his cashier. Followed the princess with twenty-three boxes and six servants. She was enormously stout, cried the whole day long, and yearned to reduce her figure.

'When the lift that was to take her down to the bath-room was not in front of her door at the very second when she left her room, she used to stamp her foot in anger, pull her maid's hair and shout:

' "What? *I* have to wait; *I*, Princess Uriassof?"

'That was the kind of patient we had. Only once there came to my floor a young fellow from the Argentine who really had something wrong with his liver. I said to him, "You are not well; you would do better to go and see a doctor."

'Towards the 24th of July the newspapers seemed to cause the noble clients of Wiesdorf sanatorium consider-able anxiety. The note to Servia, the letters they received from their homes, the clatter of arms which was beginning to be heard throughout Europe, all began to point to a vague danger which could not, of course, affect their sacred persons, but might possibly hinder them from peacefully cultivating the sufferings which were so dear to them.

'The Duchess of Broadfield telegraphed to her nephew at the Foreign Office and got no answer. Princess Uriassof began to hold mysterious confabulations with her courier.

'The German doctors soon restored every one's con-fidence; *"Unser Friedens-Kaiser . . .* our peace-loving Emperor . . . he is cruising on his yacht . . . he has not the slightest thought of war."

'The barometers of refreshment vendors are always at "set-fair," and Professor von Göteburg temporized with such authority and diplomacy that he managed to keep his international *clientèle* for another six days.

'However, the peace-loving Emperor returned only to

send threatening telegrams, and on the 27th the danger became evident even to our guests' bird-like intellects.

'Princess Uriassof announced her departure, and sent her courier to the bank to cash an enormous cheque. He came back with the message that the bank no longer cashed foreign cheques; whereupon he disappeared, and was never heard of again. The Princess was beside herself with rage, and cried that she would have him knouted. She summoned her German valet, but he was busy buckling on his *Feldwebel* uniform. She ordered her French chauffeur to be ready to start instantly; I went down to the garage with the message myself so as to get away from her, and discovered that the fellow was a reservist from Saint-Mihiel, and had left with Her Highness' car to join his regiment.

'That morning for the first time, the Duchess and the Princess condescended to notice the presence of James P. He had a magnificent 100 h.p. American car, and represented their only hope of getting across the frontier. But James P. had no more petrol, and the Germans refused to supply him with any, because his car had already been earmarked for General von Schmack's Staff.

'The same evening these first three victims of the war sat and childishly discussed the situation in an untidy room on a bed which nobody came to make. Their telegrams were no longer forwarded, their money was worthless, and the German servants in the sanatorium treated them more as prisoners than as patients. It seemed as though their fortune and their greatness had suddenly abandoned them at the first breath of war, like a slender veil torn by the wind from a woman's shoulders.

'James P. went to interview Dr von Göteburg, who answered him with ironical politeness, and depicted the pitiable plight of a Germany surrounded and attacked by a world of enemies. If, however, they were willing to leave him the princess's pearl necklace as security, he would consent to lend them the few marks they needed to cross the frontier.

'Towards midnight I entered the room where this Twilight of the Gods was drawing to an end, and saw an astounding spectacle. The Duchess of Broadfield and Princess Uriassof were attempting to pack their own trunks. Their lack of experience was only too conspicuous. In every corner there lay hats which had been crushed by their clumsy attempts; the badly folded dresses swelled awkwardly and refused with disgraceful obstinacy to allow the Princess to lock her trunks. Vanquished at last by the stress of events against which she was contending for the first time in her life, she sat down on a portmanteau and burst into tears. The Duchess, who came of a less fatalistic race, was still struggling, aided by James P., with two rebellious valises.

'I went and called Sister Therese, and with her made ready for their departure. Hoping that England would declare war, I informed the professor of my intention to accompany my patients.

'The little Alsatian girl went and asked the German servants to carry the luggage to the station for the last civilian train, which was to leave at six in the morning.

' "I don't mind carrying anything for you, *Schwester*," said the hall porter, "but I won't do a thing for those dogs of Russians and English."

'The Sister came back and said timidly, "If the doctor and Your Grace don't mind helping me, we might perhaps take at least some of these things together."

'So Wiesdorf station beheld the extraordinary sight of

[234]

the Duchess pulling an enormous portmanteau and per-spiring freely, and behind her Princess Uriassof, James P., and myself, each pushing a wheelbarrow. The station was already thronged with soldiers in *Feldgrau*. We were ravenously hungry. I asked the young Alsatian girl to accompany me to the refreshment-room, and she was able, thanks to her nurse's bonnet, to obtain two pieces of extremely dry bread from the military canteen.

'I found my patients ensconced in a fourth-class carriage. Their eyes were shut, they were leaning against the dirty wooden back of the seat, and on their faces was a smile of indescribable bliss.

'The Princess greedily seized the piece of bread I handed her, took an enormous bite out of it, and said to the Duchess:

' "What nice bread!"

' "What nice seats!" replied Her Grace, leaning voluptuously against the hard, greasy boards.'

CHAPTER XIV

THE BEGINNING OF THE END

'All the way talking of Russia, which, he says, is a sad place.'
PEPYS (Sept. 16th, 1664)

For three days our soldiers had been advancing over the devastated plain of the Somme. The crests of the innumerable shell-holes gave the country the appearance of a sort of frozen angry sea. The victors were advancing light-heartedly, as though preceded by invisible drums.

It was just at the time when the German army was swaying and tottering like a spent boxer awaiting the inevitable knock-out.

The Division had suffered heavily. All along the roads they had seen for the second time the sinister spectacle of villagers in flight and furniture-laden carts drawn by bowed women.

General Bramble had looked at the map with painful astonishment. He had been ordered to resist at all costs along the trenches on the green line; but when he reached the green line he had found no trenches; the Chinamen who were to dig them were still at sea somewhere near Suez.

Then, in a corner of a ruined village, they had come across a green felt hat and a fearsome moustache, which turned out reassuringly to belong to a rocking, tottering old man; and the Tommies—who are a primitive and

[236]

adventurous race—were glad of the protection of this wild old totem of the Frankish tribe.

Then came motor-lorries to take the whole Division to the North, and through all the bustle and disorder they were conscious of a giant hand trying with prudent and skilful movements to rebuild the line.

'What can a general do?' the doctor had asked. 'This war is too vast to be affected by human volition. Victory will come through tiny, decisive forces that have been at work since the beginning of the world. Tolstoy's Kutusoff used to go to sleep in Council—yet he beat Napoleon.'

'However vast the scale of circumstance may be,' said the colonel, 'a man can change everything. A child cannot push a railway engine; yet he can start it if he opens the right throttle. A man has only to apply his will at the right place, and he will be master of the world. Your determinism is nothing more than a paradox. You build a cage round yourself and then are astonished you are a prisoner.'

They were going forward rapidly. Aurelle, mounted on his old white Arab, trotted between the doctor and Colonel Parker.

'Don't hold your horse in so tightly, Messiou; give him the rein.'

'But the road's full of holes, sir.'

'My dear chap, when a man is on a horse, the horse is always the more intelligent of the pair.'

He slackened his mare's rein to pass by a huge shell-hole, and began to talk of the peace that was at hand.

'The most difficult thing of all,' he said, 'will be to preserve in our victory the virtues that won it for us.

Germany and Russia will do their best to corrupt us. A dishonoured nation always tries to bury its shame under the ruins of the victor's civilization. It's the device of Samson; it's as old as history itself. Rome, surrounded by vanquished and humbled nations, witnessed the lightning speed of Judaic preaching, which was so much like the Bolshevism of our day. The Russian ghettos of our capitals had their counterpart then in the Syrian dens that swarmed in the large ports; that is where the apostles of mystical communism preached most successfully. And Juvenal and Tacitus, who were gentlemen, had good reason to detest those anarchists, who condemned Roman civilization with the fanatical fury of a Trotsky.'

'Yes,' said the doctor, 'the danger of these prolonged wars is that they end by making the most unusual habits generally acceptable. They require courage; and courage is a dangerous virtue, the mother of revolutions. And it is not easy to accustom a nation of warriors to render due obedience once more to second-rate politicians and profiteers. The oligarchy of *parvenus* which arose after the Punic wars could not be respected as the Roman senate had been. They possessed neither its hardihood nor its heroic parsimony. Bent only on beautiful slaves, perfumes and luxuries, they sacrificed their nascent influence to their passion for pleasure. They did not last long.'

'It is quite certain,' the colonel continued, 'that in order to survive, an aristocracy must be hard upon itself. Moral discipline is indispensable to any class that wants to govern. If the industrial middle class is to take our place, it will have to be austere and hard. What sealed once and for all the doom of the Roman Senators was the decadent Greek culture of their sons. Those young noblemen affected an elegant dilettantism and toyed pleasantly with cultured demagogy. Caesar in his youth, Aurelle, was rather like one of your comfortable cultured French middle-class Socialists. His lifelong dream was to lead a moderate reform party, but he was embittered by the attacks of the Roman patricians. He is a type against whom our Public Schools protect us pretty well. We also have our decadent young lords, but the contempt of their own generation keeps them from doing much harm.'

He stopped in order to salute a magpie—for he was very superstitious—pointed with his cane to a tank that lay buried on its back in the sand like a defeated tortoise, and went on:

'Do you think you will have a revolution in France after the war? If you do, I shall be very much surprised. Up till now the remembrance of 1793 has kept us looking with apprehension towards France as the danger-spot of Europe. Today we realize our mistake.

'1793 made your country more conservative than any other, by giving your peasants the possession of the soil. It will probably be seen some years hence that the Russian Revolution has also had the same effect. The revolution will end when the Red armies return to Moscow and some unemployed Bonapartsky has the Soviets dispersed by his grenadiers. Then the *moujiks* who have acquired the national property will form the first layer of a respectable liberal bourgeois republic.'

'Unless,' said Aurelle, 'Bonapartsky, having tasted the sweets of victory, sets out to conquer Europe with the help of his trusty grenadiers. Between the Terror and "the respectable republic" there were twenty years of war, sir.'

'The most terrible of all revolutions,' began the doctor, 'will be the English one. In France the intellectual is popular; the tribune of the people is a bearded professor with the kindest of hearts. In England the people's commissary will be a hard, clean-shaven, silent, cruel man.'

'That may be,' said the colonel; 'but he will find more silent and still harder men up against him. If you think we are going to lie down and submit like the fatalist nobles of Petrograd, you are mistaken.'

'You, sir? And why the devil should *you* defend business men and profiteers whom you are never tired of sending to perdition?'

'I shall not be defending profiteers, but a form of society which I hold to be necessary. The institutions which our ancestors have adopted after six thousand years' experience are worth ten times more than the systems of foolish and boastful hotheads. I stand always for what is.'

With a sweeping gesture the doctor pointed to the twisted, rusty wire, the shattered walls, the mangled trees and the dense harvest of wooden crosses that rose from the barren soil.

'Allow me,' he said, 'to express the heartfelt admiration I feel for this venerable civilization of yours, and let me contemplate the fruits of these wise institutions which six thousand years have consecrated for you. Six thousand years of war, six thousand years of murder, six thousand years of misery, six thousand years of prostitution; one half of mankind busy asphyxiating the other half; famine in Europe, slavery in Asia, women sold in

the streets of Paris or London like matches or bootlaces—
there is the glorious achievement of our ancestors. It is
well worth dying to defend, I must confess!'

'Yes, doctor,' replied Aurelle; 'but there are two sides
to the question: six thousand years of reform, six thousand years of revolt, six thousand years of science, six
thousand years of philosophy——'

'Now don't you run away with the idea that I'm a
revolutionary. As far as I am concerned, the movements
of men interest me no more than those of the spiders or
the dogs I am so fond of observing. I know that all the
speeches in the world will not prevent men from being
jealous monkeys always greedy for food, females and
bright stones. It is true that they know how to deck out
their desires with a somewhat brilliant and delusive
ideology, but it is easy for an expert to recognize the
instinct beneath the thought. Every doctrine is an auto-
biography. Every philosophy demands a diagnosis. Tell
me the state of your digestion, and I shall tell you the
state of your mind.'

'Oh, doctor, if that is so, life is not worth living.'

'That, my boy, depends entirely upon the liver, as
they say.'

Young Dundas, who had just reined up level with
them, interposed:

'My God, my God,' he said, 'how you chaps do love
talking! Why, I once had a discussion myself at Oxford
with one of those johnnies in a bowler hat and ready-
made tie who go round and make speeches in public
squares on Saturday afternoons. I had stopped to listen
to him on my way back from a bathe. He was cursing
the aristocracy, the universities, and the world in general.
Well, after about five minutes' talking, I went right up

to him and said, "Off with your coat, my friend; let's go into the matter thoroughly." '

'And did you convince him, Dundas?'

'It wasn't very difficult, Messiou, because, honestly, I could use my left better than he could.'

CHAPTER XV

DANSE MACABRE

'Magical dancing still goes on in Europe today.'
SIR JAMES FRASER

'Doctor,' said General Bramble, 'this morning I received from London two new fox-trots for my gramophone.'

Ever since the Armistice sent the Scottish Division into rest on the Normandy coast, the Infant Dundas had been running a course of dancing-lessons at the mess, which were patronized by the most distinguished 'red-hats'.

Aurelle emerged from behind an unfolded copy of the *Times*.

'Things look very rotten,' he said. 'The Germans are taking heart again; you are demobbing; the Americans are sailing away; and soon only we and the Italians will be left alone to face the European chaos——'

'Aurelle,' said Colonel Parker, 'take off your coat and come and learn the one-step—that'll be a jolly sight better than sitting moping there all the evening.'

'You know I don't dance, sir.'

'You're very silly,' said Parker. 'A man who doesn't dance is an enemy of mankind. The dancer, like the bridge-player, cannot exist without a partner, so he can't help being sociable. But you—why, a book is all the company you want. You're a bad citizen.'

The doctor emptied his glass of brandy at one gulp,

[243]

removed his coat, and joined the colonel in his attack upon the young Frenchman.

'A distinguished Irish naturalist, Mr James Stephens,' he said, 'has noticed that love of dancing varies according to innocence of heart. Thus children, lambs and dogs like dancing. Policemen, lawyers and fish dance very little because they are hard-hearted. Worms and Members of Parliament, who, besides their remarkable all-round culture, have many points in common, dance but rarely owing to the thickness of the atmosphere in which they live. Frogs and high hills, if we are to believe the Bible——'

'Doctor,' interrupted the general, 'I put you in charge of the gramophone; top speed, please.'

The orderlies pushed the table into a corner, and the aide-de-camp, holding his general in a close embrace, piloted him respectfully but rhythmically round the room.

'One, two . . . one, two. It's a simple walk, sir, but a sort of glide. Your feet mustn't leave the ground.'

'Why not?' asked the general.

'It's the rule. Now twinkle.'

'Twinkle? What's that?' asked the general.

'It's a sort of hesitation, sir; you put out your left foot, then you bring it sharply back against the right, and start again with the right foot. Left, back again, and quickly right. Splendid, sir.'

The general, who was a man of precision, asked how many steps he was to count before twinkling again. The rosy-cheeked one explained that it didn't matter, you could change steps whenever you liked.

'But look here,' said General Bramble, 'how is my partner to know when I'm going to twinkle?'

'Oh,' said the aide-de-camp, 'you must hold her near

enough for her to feel the slightest movement of your body.'

'Humph!' grunted the general. And after a moment's thought he added, 'Couldn't you get up some mixed dances here?'

From the depths of the arm-chair came Aurelle's joyful approval.

'I've never been able to make out,' he said, 'what pleasure you men can find in dancing together. Dancing is a sentimental pantomime, a kind of language of the body which allows it to express an understanding which the soul dare not confess. What was dancing for primitive man? Nothing but a barbaric form of love.'

'What a really French idea!' exclaimed Colonel Parker. 'I should say rather that love is a barbaric form of dancing. Love is animal; dancing is human. It's more than an art; it's a sport.'

'Quite right,' said Aurelle. 'Since the British nation deems worthy of the name of sport any exercise which is at once useless, tiring and dangerous, I am quite ready to admit that dancing answers this definition in every way. Nevertheless, among savages——'

'Aurelle, my boy, don't talk to me about savages!' said Parker. 'You've never been out of your beloved Europe. Now I have lived among the natives of Australia and Malay; and their dances were not sentimental panto-mimes, as you call them, at all, but warlike exercises for their young soldiers, that took the place of our Swedish drill and bayonet practice. Besides, it is not so very long since these close embraces were adopted in our own countries. Your minuets and pavans were respecters of persons, and the ancients, who liked looking at dancing girls, never stooped to twirling them round.'

'That's quite easy to understand,' put in the doctor. 'What did they want with dancing? The directness of their customs made such artificial devices for personal contact quite unnecessary. It's only our Victorian austerity which makes these rhythmical embraces so attractive. Puritan America loves to waggle her hips, and——'

'Doctor,' said the general, 'turn the record over, will you, and put on speed eighty; it's a jazz.'

'What's worrying me,' began Aurelle, who had returned once more to his paper, 'is that the oracles are taking the theory of nationality so seriously. A nation is a living organism, but a nationality is nothing. Take the Jugo-Slavs, for instance——'

At that moment the doctor produced such an ear-splitting racket from the gramophone that the interpreter let his *Times* fall to the ground.

'By Jove!' he exclaimed; 'have you broken it, doctor?'

'Broken it?' repeated the doctor in mild surprise.

'You don't mean to tell me that all that noise of broken crockery and fog-horns was deliberately put together by a human brain?'

'You know nothing about it,' said the doctor. 'This negro music is excellent stuff. Negroes are much finer artists than we are; they alone can still feel the holy delirium which ranked the first singers among the gods. . . .'

His voice was drowned by the sinister racket of the jazz, which made a noise like a barrage of 4·2 howitzers in a thunderstorm.

'Jazz!' shouted the general to his aide-de-camp, bostoning majestically the while. 'Jazz—Dundas, what *is* jazz?'

[246]

'Anything you like, sir,' replied the rosy-cheeked one. 'You've just got to follow the music.'

'Humph!' said the general, much astonished.

'Doctor,' said Aurelle gravely, 'we may now be witnessing the last days of a civilization which with all its faults was not without a certain grace. Don't you think that under the circumstances there might be something better for us to do than tango awkwardly to this ear-splitting din?'

'My dear boy,' said the doctor, 'what would you do if some one stuck a pin into your leg? Well, war and peace have driven more than one spike into the hide of humanity; and of course she howls and dances with the pain. It's just a natural reflex action. Why, they had a fox-trot epidemic just like this after the Black Death in the fourteenth century; only then they called it St Vitus's dance.'

CHAPTER XVI

THE GLORY OF THE GARDEN

'But the Glory of the Garden
Lies in more than meets the eye.'
R. KIPLING

A farewell dinner was being given to Aurelle by the officers of the Scottish Division, with whom he had spent four years of danger and hardship.

Before they sat down, they made him drink a cocktail and a glass of sherry, and then an Italian vermouth tuned up with a drop of gin. Their eager affection, and this curiously un-British mixing of drinks, made him feel that on this last evening he was no longer a member of the mess, but its guest.

'I hope,' said Colonel Parker, 'that you will be a credit to the education we have given you, and that you will at last manage to empty your bottle of champagne without assistance.'

'I'll try,' said Aurelle, 'but the war has ended too soon, and I've still a lot to learn.'

'That's a fact,' grumbled the colonel. 'This damned peace has come at a most unfortunate moment. Everything was just beginning to get into shape. I had just bought a cinema for the men; our gunners were working better every day; there was a chance of my becoming a general, and Dundas was teaching me jazz. And then the politicians poke their noses in and go and make peace, and Clemenceau demobs Aurelle! Life's just one damned thing after another!'

'*Wee, Messiou*,' sighed General Bramble, 'it's a pity to see you leaving us. Can't you stay another week?'

'I'm sorry, sir, but I'm to be demobbed with the third batch, and I've got my warrant in my pocket. I'm to report tomorrow at Montreuil-sur-Mer; from there I shall be sent to Arras, and then dispatched to Versailles, after which, if I survive the journey, I shall be at liberty to return to Paris. I should be delighted to stay a few days, but I suppose I must obey the pompous military maxim and "share the fortunes of my comrades".'

'Why,' said Colonel Parker, 'are people so idiotic as to discharge soldiers whose return is dreaded by civilians and whose presence is necessary to the comfort of the Staff? We English adopted a much more intelligent plan for *our* demobilization. The men were to be classified according to their professions, and were only to be released when workmen of their occupation were required in England. In this way we were to avoid unemployment trouble. All the details were most clearly explained in a bulky volume; it was really an excellent plan. Well, when it came to be actually worked, everything went as badly as could be. Every one complained; there were small riots which were dramatized in the newspapers; and after some weeks' trial we returned to your system of classes, Aurelle, which makes for equality and is idiotic.'

'It was easy to foresee,' said the doctor, 'that any regulation which neglected human nature was bound to fail. Man, that absurd and passionate animal, cannot thrive under an intelligent system. To be acceptable to the majority a law must be unjust. The French demobilization system is inane, and that is why it is so good.'

'Doctor,' said the general, 'I cannot allow you to say that the French method is inane; this is the last evening Messiou is spending with us, and I will not have him annoyed.'

'It doesn't matter a bit,' said Aurelle; 'neither of them knows what he's talking about. It is quite true that things are going rather better in France than elsewhere, in spite of absurd decrees and orders. But that's not because our laws are unjust; it's because no one takes them seriously. In England your weakness is that if you are ordered to demobilize men by classes, you'll do it. We *say* we're doing it, but by means of all sorts of reprieves, small irregularities and reasonable injustices, we manage *not* to do it. Some barbarous bureaucrat has decreed that the interpreter Aurelle should, in order to be demobilized, accomplish the circuit Montreuil-Arras-Versailles in a cattle-truck. It is futile and vexatious; but do you suppose I shall do it? Never in your life! Tomorrow morning I shall calmly proceed to Paris by the express. I shall exhibit a paper covered with seals to a scribe at the G.M.P., who will utter a few lamentations as a matter of form, and demobilize me with much grumbling. With us the great principle of public justice is that no one is supposed to respect the laws; this is what has enabled us to beat Germany.'

'Humph!' muttered the general, much taken aback.

'Doctor,' said Colonel Parker, 'help Messiou Aurelle to some champagne; his mind is far too clear.'

Corks began to pop with the rapidity of machine-guns. Colonel Parker began a speech about the charming, kind and affectionate disposition of the women of Burma;

the doctor preferred Japanese women for technical reasons.

'French women are also very beautiful,' said General Bramble politely; for he could not forget this was Aurelle's farewell dinner.

When the orderlies had brought the port, he struck the table twice sharply with the handle of his knife, and said, with a pleasant mixture of solemnity and geniality:

'Now, gentlemen, as our friend is leaving us after having so excellently represented his country amongst us for the last four years, I propose that we drink his health with musical honours.'

All the officers stood up, glass in hand. Aurelle was about to follow their example, when Colonel Parker crushed him with a whispered, '*Assee, Messiou, poor l'amoor de Dee-er !*' And the Staff of the Scottish Division proceeded to sing with the utmost solemnity, keeping their eyes fixed upon the young Frenchman:

> '*For he's a jolly good fellow,*
> *And so say all of us. . . .*'

Aurelle was deeply moved as he gazed at the friendly faces round him, and reflected sadly that he was about to leave for ever the little world in which he had been so happy. General Bramble was standing gravely at attention, and singing as solemnly as if he were in his pew in church:

> '*For he's a jolly good fellow,*
> *And so say all of us. . . .*'

Then came much cheering, glasses were drained at a

gulp, and young, rosy-cheeked Dundas shouted, 'Speech, Messiou, speech!'

'Come, Aurelle,' said Colonel Parker, 'don't you believe you're going to get out of it as easily as all that! You must get on your hind legs, my boy, and do your bit.'

'Ah, Messiou,' said the general when the ceremony was over and the brandy had followed the port, 'I hope our two nations will remain friends after this war.'

'How could it possibly be otherwise, sir? We cannot forget——'

'The duration of our friendship,' Colonel Parker put in, 'depends neither on you, Aurelle, nor on us. The Englishman as an individual is sentimental and loyal, but he can only afford the luxury of these noble sentiments because the British nation is imbued with a holy selfishness. Albion is not perfidious, in spite of what your countrymen used to say; but she cannot tolerate the existence of a dominant power on the Continent. We love you dearly and sincerely, but if you were to discover another Napoleon . . .'

'Humph!' grunted the general, greatly shocked. 'Have some more brandy, Messiou?'

'Everything will be all right,' said the doctor cynically. 'Your cotton goods will always cost more than ours, and that is the surest guarantee of friendship.'

'Why should they cost more?' carelessly asked Aurelle, in whose brain the brandy was beginning to produce a pleasant misty feeling.

'My boy,' said the doctor, 'your Napoleon, of whom Parker is so afraid, said we were a nation of shopkeepers. We accept the compliment, and our only regret is that we are unable to return it. You have three national failings which will always prevent you from being dangerous commercial competitors: you are economical, you are simple and you are hard-working. That is what makes you a great military people; the French soldiers get accustomed to the hardship of trench life far more readily than ours. But in peace-time your very virtues betray you. In that famous woollen stocking of yours you hoard not only your francs but your initiative; and your upper classes, being content with bathrooms which our farmers would disdain, feel no call to go out and cultivate Indo-China. We never invest a penny; so our children have no alternative but to go out Empire-building. We must have comfort, which compels us to be audacious; and we are extremely lazy, which makes us ingenious.'

At this point General Bramble began to emit the series of grunting noises which invariably preceded his favourite anecdotes.

'It is quite true,' he said proudly, 'that we are lazy. One day, just after we had made an advance near Cambrai, and the position was still uncertain, I sent out an aviator to fly over a little wood and report whether the troops that occupied it were French, British or German. I watched him executing my order, and when he came back he told me the troops were British. "Are you quite certain?" I asked, "you didn't go very low." "It was not necessary, sir. I knew if those men had been busy digging trenches, I should have been uncertain whether they were French or German; but as they were sitting on the grass, I'm sure they are British." '

It was ten o'clock. The aide-de-camp poured out a whisky and soda for his general. A silence ensued, and in the kitchen close by the orderlies were heard singing the old war ditties, from 'Tipperary' to 'The Yanks are coming,' as was their nightly custom. They made a fine bass chorus, in which the officers joined unconsciously.

The singing excited Dundas, who began to yell 'view-halloos' and smack a whip he took down from the wall. The doctor found a Swiss cowbell on the mantelpiece and rang it wildly. Colonel Parker took up the tongs and began rapping out a furious fox-trot on the mantelshelf, which the general accompanied from his arm-chair with a beatific whistle.

Of the end of the evening Aurelle had but a blurred remembrance. Towards one o'clock in the morning he found himself squatting on the floor drinking stout beside a little major, who was explaining to him that he had never met more respectable women than at Port Said.

Meanwhile Dundas started to chant a ditty about the virtues of one notorious Molly O'Morgan; Colonel Parker repeated several times, 'Aurelle, my boy, don't forget that if Englishmen can afford to make fools of themselves, it is only because England is such a devilishly serious nation;' and Dr O'Grady, who was getting to the sentimental stage, sang many songs of his native land in a voice that was full of tears.

CHAPTER XVII

LETTER FROM
COLONEL PARKER TO AURELLE

'Tout homme de courage est homme de parole.'
CORNEILLE

STAPLETON HALL, STAPLETON, KENT
April —, 1920

My dear Aurelle,—Much water has passed beneath the bridges since your last letter. For one thing, I have become a farmer. When I left my staff job I thought of rejoining my old regiment; but it wasn't easy, as the battalion is crammed full of former generals who are only subalterns.

They are treating the army very unfairly here. Our damned Parliament refuses to vote it any money; very little is required of it, it's true—it has merely to maintain order in Ireland and to guard the Rhine, Mesopotamia, India, Egypt, Turkey, Palestine, Silesia, the Caucasus and a few other countries the names of which I can't remember! All I can say is, God help England!

We farmers also can do with His help. April is the month for sowing, and fine weather is necessary. As far as I am concerned, I had a hundred acres of potatoes to sow, and I had made detailed preparations for my spring offensive. But, as always happens when the poor British start attacking, rain began falling in bucketfuls the very first day of operations. The advance had to be stopped after a few acres, and public opinion is really much exercised about the matter.

Now I want to answer your letter. You say, 'Some of you in England seem astonished that we refuse to trust the Germans. We are accused of a lack of generosity. What a splendid piece of unconscious humour! I'd like to see you in our shoes—suppose there were no sea between those chaps and yourselves!'

My dear Aurelle, I have often asked you not to confuse the English people with their cursed Puritans. There have always been in this country a large number of men who have done their best to destroy the strength and reputation of our Empire. Up to the time of good Queen Bess, these scoundrels were kept in their place, and I often regret I was not born in those times. Since then the Puritan element has on every occasion displayed its narrow-mindedness and its hatred of patriotism and of everything beautiful and joyous. The Puritans prefer their opinions to their country, which is an abominable heresy. They brought the civil wars upon us at the time of the Stuarts; they helped the rebels during the American War of Independence and the French during their Revolution. They were pro-Boers in the South African War, conscientious objectors in this one, and now they are supporting the republican murderers in Ireland, trying to undermine the British workman's faith in his King and county cricket, and doing their best to encourage the Germans by creating difficulties between France and ourselves.

But you must not forget that the magnificent in-difference and ignorance of our race makes these pedants quite harmless.

You ask me what the average British citizen thinks about it all. Well, I'm going to tell you.

What interests the average British citizen beyond everything is the match between England and Scotland, which is to be played next Saturday at Twickenham, the Grand National, which is to be run next week at Liverpool, and Mrs Bamberger's divorce, which fills the newspapers just now.

What does the British citizen think? Well, he went to the war without knowing what it was all about, and he has come back from it without having gathered any further information. As a matter of fact, he is beginning to wonder who won it. You say it was Foch, and we are quite ready to believe you; still, it seems to us that our army had a little to do with it. The Italians say *they* struck the decisive blow; so do the Serbians and the Portuguese, of course. The Americans go about wearing little badges in their buttonholes which proclaim, '*We* did it.' Ludendorff claims that the German army won the war. I am beginning to ask myself whether *I* was not the victor. As a matter of fact, I'm inclined to think it was you. You kept the Infant Dundas quiet; if you hadn't repressed him, he would have kept General Bramble from working; the general would have been nervous at the time of the attack in April '18, and all would have been lost.

As to international politics I have very little to tell you. I am observing the bucolic mind, and am noticing with some anxiety that the brain of the countryman is very much like the turnip he grows with such perseverance. I am hoping I shall not also develop any vegetable characteristics.

You ask whether we are forgetting France. I don't

think we are. Do you know that we were ready to remit your war debts if America had agreed? Not so bad for a nation of shopkeepers, is it? We don't brag about our devotion, but we will be with you if anything goes wrong. I trust you know us well enough to be quite assured of that.

I am very busy this morning with my favourite sow, who has just borne a litter of twelve. She immediately squashed one of them; King Solomon was not such a clever judge as he looked after all. Au revoir.

CHAPTER XVIII

GENERAL BRAMBLE'S RETURN

'The English have a mild aspect and a ringing, cheerful voice.'
EMERSON

'By Jove,' said the Infant Dundas, 'this Paris of yours *is* a jolly town.'

Beltara the painter had invited Aurelle to spend an evening in his studio to meet General Bramble, who was passing through Paris on his way to Constantinople, accompanied by Dundas and Dr O'Grady.

The general was sitting on a divan piled high with many-coloured cushions, and gazing with emotion upon the sketch of a nude figure. The Greek heads, Etruscan warriors and Egyptian scribes about him had the rare and spiritual beauty of mutilated things. Aurelle gazed at his old chief as he sat motionless among the statues, and consecrated the brief moment of silence to the memory of his virtues.

'A fine woman,' exclaimed the general, 'a very fine woman indeed! What a pity I can't show you a few Sudan negresses, Beltara!'

Beltara interrupted him to introduce one of his friends, Lieutenant Vincent, a gunner with a frank, open face. The general, fixing his clear gaze on Aurelle, tried to speak of France and England.

'I'm glad, Messiou, that we've come to an understand-

[259]

ing at last. I'm not very well up in all this business, but I can't stand all these bickering politicians.'

Aurelle was suddenly conscious of the general's real sincerity and anxiety about the future. Lieutenant Vincent came up to them. He had the rather wild, attractive grace of the present-day youth. As he sat listening to General Bramble's words about English friendship, his lips parted as though he was burning to break in.

'Will you allow me, sir,' he suddenly interrupted, 'to tell you how we look at it. Frankly speaking, you English were marvellous during the war, but since the Armistice you have been on the wrong tack entirely. You are on the wrong tack because you don't know the Germans. Now I've just come back from Germany, and it is absolutely clear that as soon as those fellows have enough to eat they'll fall on us again. *You* want to get their forgiveness for your victory. But why should they accept their defeat? Would you accept it in their place?'

'The sense of shame after victory,' said the doctor gently, 'is a sentiment quite natural to barbarous peoples. After employing the utmost cruelty during the fight, they come and implore their slaughtered enemies' pardon. "Don't bear us a grudge for having cut off your heads," they say; "if we had been less lucky you would have cut off ours." The English always go in for this kind of posthumous politeness. They call it behaving like sportsmen. It's really a survival of the "enemy's taboo".'

'It would be quite all right,' put in Lieutenant Vincent breathlessly, 'if you waited to appease the shades of your enemies till you were quite certain they were really dead. But the Germans are very much alive. Please understand, sir, that I'm speaking absolutely without hate. What I mean is that we must destroy Carthage—that is German military power—so completely that the very idea of revenge will appear absurd to any German with an ounce of common sense. As long as there exists at any time the barest chance of an enterprise, they will attempt it. I don't blame them in the least for it; in fact I admire them for not despairing of their country; but our duty—and yours too—is to make such an enterprise impossible.'

'Yes,' said the general in rather feeble French; 'but you can't hit a man when he's down, can you?'

'It's not a question of being down, sir. Do you know that the three big gunpowder factories in Germany pay a dividend of fifteen per cent? Do you know that Krupp is building a factory in Finland in order to escape our supervision? Do you realize that in ten years, if we don't keep an eye on their chemical factories, the Germans will be able to wage a frightful war against us, and use methods of which we haven't the slightest inkling? Now why should we run this risk when we are clearly in a position to take all precautions for some years to come? Carthage *must* be destroyed, sir. Why, just look at Silesia. . . .'

'Every one's talking about Silesia,' said the Infant Dundas. 'What *is* it, really?'

Vincent, waving his arms despairingly, went to the piano and played a long, sad phrase of Borodin, the one which is sung by the recumbent woman just before Prince Igor's dances. Before Aurelle's eyes floated Northern landscapes, muddy fields and bleeding faces, mingling with the women's bare shoulders and the silk embroideries in the studio. He was suddenly seized by a healthy emotion, like a breath of fresh air, which made him want to ride across the wide world beside General Bramble.

'Doctor, can't we remain "musketeers"?' he said.

'Can't be done,' said the doctor sarcastically, 'till this damned peace ends.'

'You hateful person!' said Beltara. 'Will you have a whisky and soda?'

'What!' exclaimed the general joyfully, 'you've got whisky in the house, here, in France?'

'It is pleasant to notice,' said the doctor, 'that the war has been of some use after all. Your whisky, Beltara, quite reassures me about the League of Nations. As the Entente is necessary to the safety of our two countries, the responsibility of preserving good relations ought to be given to doctors and psychologists. Such experts would make it their business to cultivate those sentiments which tend to unite two countries into one. They would remind people, by means of noise and military cere- monies, of the great things they had achieved together. England would be represented at these functions, as she is in the minds of most Frenchmen, by Scotchmen and Australians. Bagpipes, kilts, bugles and tam-o'-shanters are far better diplomatists than ambassadors are. Pageants, dances, a few sentimental anecdotes, exchanges of song, common sports, common drinks—these are the essence of a good international policy. The Church, which is always so wise and so human, attaches as much importance to works as to faith. The outward signs of friendship are much more important than friendship itself, because they are sufficient to support it.'

'Beltara,' said the general, 'will you ask your friend to play the "Destiny Waltz" for Messiou?'

Once more the familiar strains rang out, and brought